"Please don't do that, Blue," Cassie begged.

"What?"

"Rub my back like that."

"It feels good, doesn't it? Does it feel *too* good, Cassie?"

Her name sounded like a velvet whisper on his lips. She suddenly realized she was trembling from head to toe. He had not only kissed her, he'd kissed her good.

Blue followed her into the kitchen. "I could gobble you up."

She didn't doubt it for a second. His eyes were filled with desire. "This isn't going to work if I have to run from you."

"You're running in circles, you know. If I wanted to, I'd take you without a second thought."

"What's stopping you, then?" she asked defiantly.

"Because I'm a patient man. I'll wait for you to come to me."

"That'll be the day, Blue Mitchum."

"Answer one question—was the kiss all you expected?"

Cassie sighed. She couldn't look into his stark blue eyes and lie. "Yes, it was good. Better than I expected. Which is why it'll never happen again."

Blue smiled, "Never say never. You need to be kissed, and often. And when you're ready, I'll take you to the moon. . . ."

WHAT ARE *LOVESWEPT* ROMANCES?

They are stories of true romance and touching emotion. We believe those two very important ingredients are constants in our highly sensual and very believable stories in the *LOVESWEPT* line. Our goal is to give you, the reader, stories of consistently high quality that may sometimes make you laugh, sometimes make you cry, but are always fresh and creative and contain many delightful surprises within their pages.

Most romance fans read an enormous number of books. Those they truly love, they keep. Others may be traded with friends and soon forgotten. We hope that each *LOVESWEPT* romance will be a treasure—a "keeper." We will always try to publish

LOVE STORIES YOU'LL NEVER FORGET
BY AUTHORS YOU'LL ALWAYS REMEMBER

The Editors

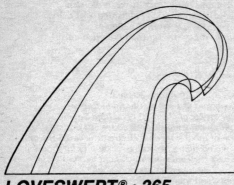

LOVESWEPT® • 365
Charlotte Hughes
Scoundrel

BANTAM BOOKS
NEW YORK • TORONTO • LONDON • SYDNEY • AUCKLAND

SCOUNDREL

A Bantam Book / November 1989

ISBN 0-553-22038-1

To Catherine, with love

"Mommy, why are you smiling?" six-year-old Bree asked, her blond ringlets bouncing against her shoulder as she spoke.

"Shhh!" her sister, Tara, said, her nose pressed close to the small television set in one corner of the car as she watched a Tom and Jerry cartoon. "Can't you shut up *ever*?" Tara asked. In response, Bree stuck out her tongue.

Cassie leaned over to Bree and whispered, "I'm smiling because I can't wait to see the looks on the faces of everyone in my family when we pull up in front of the house. It's been so long since I've seen them." Too long, she thought. The girls had been babies. But Jean-François had always kept her on such a tight schedule . . . Looking back, she could see it had been intentional. He had purposely tried to alienate her from her family.

Cassie realized that dwelling on her failed marriage would get her nowhere. After learning Jean-François had filtered funds into private bank accounts—money she had made sitting under hot lights for hours or posing until she'd thought she would drop—after spending almost two years battling with him in a courtroom, the pain was gone.

At the age of thirty, Cassandra D'Clair was still one of the most-sought-after models in the business. The black skirt and gray-and-black houndstooth jacket she wore were her own designs. Her ash-blond hair, streaked by a stylist who worked exclusively with actresses and models, was pulled into a demure bun at the nape of her neck. Wispy tendrils of hair strayed from the bun, defying the prim hairstyle she'd arranged.

"Driver, you can stop when you reach the farm-house on the left," Cassie said, trying to contain her excitement.

"Mommy, is this where our new grandma lives?" Bree asked, bouncing on the seat, obviously tired of being confined. Tara sat quietly, as though it were the grown-up thing to do. The chauffeur pulled into the drive and parked.

Cassie nodded. "Stay in the car," she said. "I'll see if anyone is home." The driver got out and opened her door.

The place looked much the same as Cassie remembered, but then, she realized, her parents had always taken pride in their small farm, despite the fact that they had to work full time in the mill as well. Although Cassie possessed the means to support them for the rest of their lives, both her mother and father had made it plain in the beginning that they would not take her money.

Cassie made her way up the steps to the front porch and knocked on the door. A tall, bearded man answered. "Hello," she said in surprise. "I'm looking for the Kennards. I'm their daughter Cassie."

"I know who you are," the man said, looking genuinely impressed. "I reckon your face has been in pert near every magazine I've seen." He stroked his beard thoughtfully. "Your folks went camping somewhere in Florida. Left day before yesterday. The whole family went. Looked like a caravan goin' down the road."

Cassie felt a stab of disappointment. "How long do they plan to be gone?" she asked.

"Till the end of the month. Me and the missus needed a place to stay until our house is painted, so we agreed to keep an eye on the place and feed the livestock. Did your folks know you were coming?"

Cassie shook her head. "I wanted to surprise them," she said, doing some mental arithmetic. "That means they won't be back for seventeen days," she added dully. Her family had always gone camping the last couple of weeks before school started. How could she have forgotten? That proved how far apart they'd grown since she'd moved away.

"I reckon you could stay here," the man offered. "I'm sure we could make room."

Cassie pondered his suggestion. She wouldn't feel comfortable staying with perfect strangers, even if it was her parents' house.

"That won't be necessary," Cassie finally said. "I have a place to stay," she added, hoping she was correct in that assumption. "But thanks for your help." She made her way back to the limo with the bearded man in tow. She forced herself to smile as the chauffeur opened the door for her. "If my folks call to check on the place, don't tell them I'm here," she said to the man, knowing they would cut short their trip. "I want to surprise them." He nodded, his gaze fixed on the limo.

Cassie climbed into the car, thankful to be out of the heat. The driver closed the door and took his place at the wheel. He waited for instructions. "Turn right once you back out of the drive, please," Cassie told him.

"Mommy, isn't Grandma home?" Bree asked.

"No, everybody went camping until the end of the month," Cassie said, trying to keep the disappointment out of her voice. "But that will give us time to move into our new house."

Cassie gave the driver directions to the house she'd recently purchased. Twenty minutes later he pulled the limo into the driveway. At the sight of the house, Cassie's mouth fell open in surprise, and she stared a full minute before saying anything.

"Just leave the luggage on the front porch," she told the man as he helped her out of the car. The chauffeur unloaded their luggage, muttering that it looked like enough for four families, and set the bags on the porch. Cassie tipped him generously and thanked him. A moment later the black limo pulled onto the dirt road, sending a ball of dust in its wake.

Suddenly she wondered whether she'd made a terrible mistake. Her head ached, the girls were tired, and if the house was in as bad repair on the inside as it was on the outside, she wasn't sure they could stay.

Cassie and her daughters stood looking at the house. "I used to ride by this house every day on the school bus when I was a little girl," Cassie said, shaking her head in disbelief. "I always dreamed of living here."

"Did it have windows then?" Tara asked.

"Yes. This house used to be a showplace in its day."

Neither girl looked impressed, and Cassie didn't blame them. The house had been built sometime around 1890 to resemble an antebellum home, she remembered, but now the tall wrought-iron fence surrounding the mansion needed painting, and the gate hung open on one hinge, and the structure was dilapidated.

"It looks like that house on *The Adams Family*," Bree said.

Cassie's face drooped like a day-old lily, and, seeing their mother's expression, both girls decided it was time to do some exploring.

"Don't go far," Cassie warned. "And stay out of the barn until I've seen it for myself. The wood might be rotted. And be careful to watch for snakes—" Cassie caught herself. Good grief, she thought, she was beginning to sound neurotic. She would have to stop being so overprotective. Her life as a model had been rewarding in many ways, but because she was often called away from home, the girls had had a full-time nanny. She realized she had a lot to learn about being a mother, but she'd never looked forward to anything more.

Cassie took a deep breath. No matter how bad the place looked at the moment, this was her house. She was finally free. She studied the front with a critical eye. The place would definitely need painting. The four stately columns had begun to peel long ago, as had the rest of the exterior. The intricate wood molding that adorned the house was chipped in places. One shutter looked as though it might fall with the slightest breeze, and several others were missing. She would have to hire a gardener, she thought, noting the overgrown hedges and weed-infested flowerbeds. But the giant oaks made Cassie smile. The gnarled limbs seemed to reach out in welcome.

Cassie reached into her purse and fumbled for the keys the realtor had mailed to her some weeks before. She walked up the steps leading to the front porch and paused a second before trying one. Opening the door, she stepped into the foyer. A free-floating staircase, minus several balusters, dominated the room. Various doors opened off the hall, enticing Cassie to investigate.

The wood floors were warped and bowed in places from dampness. Cassie sighed wearily when she saw an ugly water stain blotting a large section of one ceiling. The paint had faded over the years so that it was impossible to tell what color the walls had been. But as she walked she envisioned how they'd look painted a soft salmon color, the elaborate woodwork and crown molding painted ivory.

She continued her tour, paling at the sight of the kitchen. The place didn't need a face-lift, as the realtor had said, it needed to be torn down and rebuilt. The cabinet doors in the kitchen literally hung from their hinges. The appliances were useless. The linoleum on the countertop was cut and torn so badly, it was obvious the house had been vandalized. The sink was so badly stained, she didn't think it would ever come clean. Everything was a mess, and Cassie realized it was going to cost a small fortune to make the place livable. "We can't live here," she said aloud, her decision final.

"Why not?" a male voice asked from the doorway. "Of course, the neighbors will talk, but since I'm your only neighbor for miles, it really doesn't matter."

Cassie felt as if her heart had slammed into her throat. She whirled around at the sound of the voice.

"Blue Mitchum," she said in a stilted and disbelieving tone.

He had matured over the years, but time had been good to him, had enhanced his looks. His waist was trim, his thighs and hips lean but finely muscled in a pair of shamefully tight denims. A cigarette dangled from his mouth in a careless manner as his gaze moved slowly and insolently over her body. His face was unshaved, and he looked as though he'd just crawled out of some woman's bed. A cotton workshirt hung open to his waist and displayed the coarse black hair on his chest. The short sleeves offered a view of taut biceps. Beads of sweat trickled down his breastbone. He made her think of a young Marlon Brando. Cassie tried not to stare, but she'd never been able to control her reaction to him—and it had always irritated her.

Blue pulled the cigarette from his mouth, ignoring the ashes that wafted to the floor. His smile was slow in coming, and there was a hint of surprise in his stark blue eyes. His stance was cocky, bordering on belligerent. "Well, I'll be damned if it isn't little Cassie Kennard all grown up." And looking like a million bucks, he added silently. "What brings you home? Did somebody die?"

His sarcastic remark only confirmed to her that

he hadn't changed one iota over the years. "I've moved back," she said with a forced smile, intent on starting off on the right foot with him.

"Getting too old to model bikinis, eh?"

"Courtesy was always one of your finer qualities, Blue. It's what I remember most about you," she said in reply, surprised that he could still raise her ire.

He hooked his thumb over his belt and gave her a smile she was sure had sent many hearts aflutter. "So you thought of me. I'm flattered."

"I figured you would be."

"You plan on living here?" He studied his surroundings.

"I had planned on living here until I saw all the work that needs to be done." Cassie felt weak in the knees, and she didn't know if it was because of the heat or the fact that she'd come face-to-face with the notorious Blue Mitchum. As sunlight slanted through the kitchen window, bringing out the highlights in his hair, she recalled why his schoolmates had tagged him "Blue." But it wasn't his blue-black hair that had fascinated her, it was the stark blue eyes that looked out-of-place against his dark coloring. "What are you doing here?" she asked.

"I saw the hearse leave. I figured the governor was in town. I'm glad it wasn't him—you're better-looking." The lopsided grin he gave her displayed his perfect white teeth and was probably the same grin he'd used to entice girls into the back seat of his car years before, she thought.

Cassie didn't know how to respond. Blue Mitchum

had always been an enigma. She still remembered how he used to race up and down the main street of Peculiar in his old Ford. It was rumored he used the back of the car more than the front. Every girl he'd dated had earned a bad reputation as a result. Still, Cassie had often wondered what it would be like to be kissed by Blue Mitchum. At the time, it seemed terribly naughty even to think such a thing. Younger than Blue by four or five years, she hadn't run with his crowd. She'd been a shy teenager with only a few close friends, but she'd had an active fantasy life, and he'd played a major role in it.

Blue swaggered over to the sink and tossed his cigarette into it. He leaned against the counter next to her and crossed his legs. He folded his arms over his powerful chest. One arm brushed hers. "You got a set of wheels?"

His touch, though light as a feather, sent tingles from her shoulder to her elbow. Cassie inched away. When she merely shook her head, he tossed her a beguiling smile.

"How do you plan to get around? We don't have a limousine service in town."

Cassie smiled at his remark. She would show the man that he no longer had the power to rattle her. She wasn't the demure adolescent she had been once. "I expected my parents to be home. I just learned they went camping, and that friends of theirs are staying in their house. Her voice sounded edgy. Blue would rejoice if he knew how uneasy he made her, had *always* made her. "I'll have to buy a car right away, but at the moment

I'm more concerned with where we're going to stay."

"We? Are you traveling with your entourage?"

As if in answer to his question, the back door flew open, and Tara stood there gasping for breath. She barely noticed Blue. "Bree's hurt," she said. "I was swinging her on a tire swing in the backyard, and the rope broke."

Cassie ran out the door before Tara could finish her sentence. Blue followed. Finding her daughter spread-eagled on the ground, she leaned over her, wondering if she should try to move the child. Bree's bones could be broken, she knew.

"Honey, Mommy's here now," Cassie said above her daughter's crying. She brushed the blond strands away from the little girl's forehead. "Can you speak to me?"

Bree answered with a sob and a grunt.

Blue knelt beside them. "The fall just knocked the breath out of her, that's all." He smiled at Bree. "Don't be scared, Curly Locks, it'll come back."

Cassie was almost hysterical as she watched her daughter gasp for air. "Shouldn't we do something?"

Blue was calm and in control. "Okay, see if you can take a deep breath now," he told Bree. "No? Okay, how about an itsy-bitsy one?" he asked, holding his thumb and forefinger close together. Cassie watched, her own breath coming in little gasps as her daughter's slowly returned to normal. She closed her eyes in relief.

"See, you're going to be okay," Blue assured

her, helping Bree sit up. "Tell me what hurts, kiddo, and we'll fix it."

"Th-the back of my . . . head," Bree said, struggling to speak. "And my behind."

Tara's hands flew to her mouth as she gaped at her mother. "Did you hear Bree talk about her privates in front of a stranger?"

"Is she okay?" Cassie asked anxiously, hugging Tara to her side.

Blue nodded as he checked for broken bones. "Yeah. She's not bleeding, but there's a bump on her head. She could use an ice pack."

Cassie looked around helplessly. She sighed her frustration. "Nothing has gone right since we got here," she said.

"We can take her to my house," Blue said. "I live just down the road. My jeep is out front."

"Your house?" Cassie echoed in a voice that told him she was reluctant to go.

Blue lifted Bree gently. "Don't worry," he said, leaning over to whisper in Cassie's ear. "I'll get rid of the drug smugglers and hookers before you come in."

"That's not what I meant," she said, blushing. Actually, she was grateful for his help, but that didn't mean that his presence wasn't disconcerting.

Blue lifted Bree very carefully and carried her around the house to where his jeep was parked in the driveway. He set her down gently in the back seat, then helped Tara in. "What in the world is all that?" he said, motioning toward the Gucci bags on the front porch.

Cassie blanched. "Our luggage."

"What do you do, change clothes every time you go to the bathroom?" He didn't wait for a reply. "Well, we'll have to take it. This place has been broken into a couple of times by teenagers. You lock up, and I'll try to get this stuff in the jeep. And hurry before the knot on this kid's head grows to the size of a chicken egg." Ugly luggage, he thought as he tossed the bags into a storage area at the back of the jeep. Surely she could afford Samsonite.

Cassie couldn't seem to pry her eyes off the man's body. The way his jeans hugged his hips and molded to his thighs made her mouth go dry. The buttons on his shirt literally strained against his wide chest. Was he still the unsavory character he'd been in his youth, she wondered. Without wasting another second, she scurried into the house and picked up her purse and keys. She hurried out the front door and locked it. Blue had already loaded most of the luggage. "Uh . . . Blue?" She hesitated. "On second thought, perhaps we should go to a motel."

"The Shady Lane?" He laughed as he tried to squeeze a bag between Tara's feet and the back of his seat. "The fire marshal closed that place down years ago. Just get in the jeep, prissy britches."

Cassie had the odd feeling he was making fun of her. "If we're going to resort to name-calling—"

"I'll just bet you've got a couple picked out for me, right?" He grinned.

Tossing him a dirty look, she climbed into the jeep. Prissy britches indeed! Who did he think he was, for heaven's sake? Blue cranked the engine, shifted gears, and off they shot. Cassie held on tight. She glanced back at the girls. "Hold on," she warned as the vehicle bounced along the dirt road. "Mr. Mitchum has spent his life practicing to become a race-car driver." The girls laughed in delight. Blue merely smiled.

Cassie turned around in her seat and contemplated their next move. Once she attended to Bree's bump, she'd have to figure out where they could go. They wouldn't stay at Blue's place any longer than absolutely necessary. His effect on her was too potent. Cassie shot him a sidelong glance. She had always been intrigued by the tales surrounding him. Some said he was the illegitimate son of a Choctaw chieftain, which accounted for his dark coloring. It had been rumored that Blue's mother had met his father while doing social work on an Indian reservation in North Carolina. She'd come home to have the baby and scandalized her family. A frail wisp of a woman, she had died in childbirth, leaving Blue to be raised by unloving grandparents. Cassie couldn't count the times she had dreamed about him. Even now, his brooding eyes made her heart beat faster.

Cassie watched Blue shift gears, and his hands captured her attention. They were dark like the rest of him and feathered with the same black hair. There was an inherent strength in his hands. She had noticed calluses earlier, which meant he was used to hard work. Still, he'd been surprisingly gentle with Bree. Her gaze lingered on his face. It was handsome but stern. Although his eyes were one of his assets, they were forever watchful, a bit distrustful. His full bottom lip was downright sexy. Blue suddenly glanced in her direction and caught her staring. Cassie's cheeks burned as he shot her a like-what-you-see? look, and she had the sudden urge to bail out of the fast-moving jeep. The man very obviously thought he was God's gift to the female gender.

Minutes later they pulled up in front of Blue's house. It was a two-story farmhouse, which boasted a new coat of white paint.

"This used to be old man Trotter's place," Cassie said in surprise.

"Not anymore," Blue said matter-of-factly.

"What are you doing living here?"

"My tepee burned." When he saw the look she shot him, he chuckled. "I bought it for a song after Trotter died. Nobody else would have the place." He parked the jeep under a group of tall oaks that shaded the front yard. A golden retriever lumbered over to the jeep, wagging his tail. "Hello, Duke," Blue said once he'd climbed out. "We got company."

"Will he bite?" Tara asked anxiously.

"Naw, Duke loves kids, don't you, boy?" He patted the dog on the head.

"Can I play with him?" Bree asked.

Blue helped Tara out of the jeep and swept Bree up in his arms once more. "First things first, young lady. Once we get that bump taken care of, you can play with Duke all you like. I'll even teach you to make him sing."

Bree's eyes became wide as saucers. "He can sing?"

"Dogs can't sing," Tara mumbled doubtfully.

Blue shrugged. "Duke can, in a roundabout way. He thinks he's part hound dog. I wouldn't enter him in a talent show, though. He's a little off-key."

A short time later, Cassie was holding a home-made ice pack to Bree's head and sipping iced tea while taking covert glances at her neat surroundings. Though much of the furniture in the house was old, Blue had restored the pieces to their natural beauty. Her gaze came to rest on a solitary picture hanging on one wall.

"Is that a picture of your mother?" Cassie asked.

He nodded without commenting on it. "Okay, girls, here are your cold drinks." Blue had made the girls a cherry drink from a powdered mix, which had surprised Cassie as much as seeing his clean house. The last thing she would have expected to find in Blue Mitchum's cabinets was a box of children's drink mix. He looked like a Budweiser man, crushed beer can and all.

Cassie pondered their dilemma. They had to find someplace to stay. Even though Blue had been a perfect gentleman since Bree's accident, Cassie would have been blind to miss the looks he gave her—as if she were breakfast, and he was about to dig in.

"Mommy, I'm hungry," Bree announced when Cassie removed the ice pack a half-hour later. The knot on her head had gone down considerably.

Cassie blushed, hoping Blue hadn't heard. "Shhh. I'll feed you as soon as I can."

"Tell you what," Blue said, as though trying to change the subject. "If you girls will check right inside the barn, you'll find a box full of newborn kittens."

Bree and Tara shrieked with delight as they headed for the back door, but Cassie stopped Bree. "Take it easy, okay? You just hit your head. No running." Once she'd extracted a promise from the girl, Cassie watched from the window as her two daughters headed in the direction of the barn. When they were out of sight, she turned back around. Suddenly the room seemed to shrink in size as Blue and Cassie gazed at each other in silence.

"I'm not a great cook," he finally said, "but I *do* know how to grill hamburgers."

"Oh, I couldn't impose." An inner voice told Cassie to gather her daughters and leave, now that Bree was okay. The Blue Mitchum she'd once known had stirred up her senses, but the new-and-improved Blue was doing things to her she'd never guessed were possible. If only she had rented a car instead of taking the limo her secretary had arranged. But because of her foolish pride she'd wanted to come home in style. She made a silent vow to be strong.

"No imposition. I'll light the grill and take a quick shower while it heats." He noticed she seemed to be taking a long time to decide. "Look, Cassie, I'm not going to scalp you or burn your girls at the stake. That went out centuries ago."

"What makes you say things like that?" she asked, wondering how he'd react if he knew what she'd really like him to do to her.

"Something I learned a long time ago." He

shrugged. "Why do you seem so . . . so uncomfortable around me? The worst that can happen is that I'll carry you off to shower with me."

She blushed. Even though the wicked grin on his face told her he was teasing, the thought of standing naked in a shower with Blue Mitchum did a number on her central nervous system. She tried to smile. "I appreciate your offer—of dinner, I mean," she added quickly, wishing he wouldn't look at her with those . . . eyes. "But . . ." She paused. But what? What was her alternative? She sighed, too tired to put up a fight? "What can I do to help?"

"You can kick your shoes off, plop yourself in that recliner, and make those worry lines disappear. Didn't they warn you about those in modeling school?"

Before Cassie realized what was happening, Blue sat her in a chair, knelt before her, and removed her high heels. "I don't know how you women wear these things," he muttered, glancing at the spike heels. "Seems to me it would be worse than giving birth." He began to gently massage one foot with his big hands while Cassie sat frozen in place with her mouth agape. Her tongue was literally plastered to the roof of her mouth as though it were being held by a big glob of peanut butter.

" 'Course, there's nothing sexier than a woman in high heels if her legs are shapely. And yours fill the bill. I've seen you in enough lingerie ads to know. The rest I've left to my vivid imagination."

Cassie knew she should put a halt to the foot rub and the conversation, but the sensations were so wonderful, she couldn't help but enjoy them. Her feet had ached all day, until she was certain the new heels would cripple her for life. She felt as though she were being hypnotized, his touch seeming to pull her deeper and deeper into relaxation. Blue's fingers worked out the soreness with slow deliberate strokes that sent tingles up the soles of her feet to her calves.

"Are these real silk?"

Cassie blinked. "What?"

"Your stockings. Are they the real thing?"

She nodded dumbly, happy she'd worn the expensive hose. "The girls," Cassie said absently, remembering her children were in the barn.

"They're okay. I keep all my tools put away."

Cassie closed her eyes. "I'm a sucker for a foot rub or a massage."

The smile he gave her would have sent her running had her eyes been open. "I'll keep that in mind. Now, why don't you move over to that sofa and take a quick nap before dinner. I'll check the girls before I jump in the shower. Unless you want to join me."

Her eyes shot open. "No!"

He shrugged. "Maybe next time."

"That's not likely." Her heart was beating erratically.

"Same ol' Cassie."

"What's that supposed to mean?"

He dropped his gaze to her mouth. "You always were a goody-two-shoes." He paused briefly. "Or maybe you just thought you were too good for a half-breed."

"You have a chip on your shoulder, Blue," she heard herself say. "I'm surprised you've been able to carry it around all these years."

He acted as though he hadn't heard her. "Has stardom changed you, *Mrs.* D'Clair, or are you still the prim-and-proper girl I knew long ago who wore knee socks and pigtails and didn't shave her legs until she was in high school?"

She ignored his taunting, although she couldn't help but wonder how he knew when she had started shaving her legs. "I'm not a prude, and I'm divorced now," she said coolly.

"So I heard. Did you suddenly develop an aversion to old men?"

Cassie jumped from her seat. "I don't have to listen to this." She regretted her move instantly. It put her face-to-face with him. She could actually feel the heat emanating from his body. He wore no cologne—his scent was purely masculine.

"Perhaps you should try a younger man. One with staying power."

"You're uncivilized," she said in a tight voice.

He grinned. "I know. That's what makes it so much fun to be around people like you."

"You're just holding a grudge because I never climbed in the back of your station wagon with you."

"But you thought about it."

"Never," she lied.

The look he gave her was knowing. "Oh, yes, you did. But somebody obviously made you think your virginity was sacred." He shrugged indifferently. "Which is just as well, because I never messed with virgins."

Cassie gritted her teeth but maintained her composure. "Would you kindly drive my daughters and me to the next town, where we can find lodging?" she said politely. "I'm willing to pay you well for your trouble."

"In money?"

"Of course in money," she said as she stepped into her high heels. "If you won't take us, I'll call the sheriff and have a deputy drive us." She knew from experience that taxicabs didn't exist in Peculiar.

Blue looked as though she'd just slapped him in the face. He studied her for a moment. "I guess you're not like most women I know, Cassie," he said, his expression dazed. "Look, I'm sorry for being such a son of a bitch, but I just wasn't prepared for the grown-up version of Cassie Kennard."

Cassie was about as prepared for his apology as she was for a blizzard in midsummer. She glanced down at her shoes, not knowing what to do or say. Perhaps this was just another one of Blue's seduction tactics. Confuse a woman, then make his move.

"I guess I still hold a few grudges," he confessed.

She looked up in bewilderment. "Meaning?"

"I was good enough to do odd jobs for your folks, but I wasn't good enough to invite to dinner. Your mother used to hand me a cold drink out the back door rather than invite me in to cool off." He paused. "And you used to snub me as if I were week-old garbage."

"I never snubbed you!" Cassie said defensively.

"You always looked the other way when we passed."

"Because you were older and a bit frightening. I didn't know what to say to you."

"Naw, you were too caught up in cheerleading and hanging around the jocks, the guys with the right clothes and enough money to spend on you."

"That's not fair. I always admired you in a way for being such a . . . free spirit. But I was raised differently. As for my parents and the rest of the folks in this town, they were probably afraid of you."

He gave a snort of a laugh. "Afraid?"

"Yes, afraid. Afraid of your drinking, your cussing, the way you burned rubber every time you climbed behind the wheel of your car. You were every mother's nightmare where daughters were concerned. And the gang you hung out with—" She stopped, wondering if she'd said too much. What would the infamous Blue Mitchum do if he lost his temper?

Blue ran his fingers through his thick hair. "You're not telling me anything I don't already know." At least she was honest. Cassie Kennard had been taught morals, something his grandparents had never had time to teach him. His grandfather had waited until he slipped up, then had beat the daylights out of him. "Stay for dinner, Cassie," he said gently. "I'll try to behave myself."

He glanced out the window. "Go ahead and put your feet up. I'll check the girls."

Cassie started to decline, but the truth of the matter was, she was downright exhausted. It hadn't been easy traveling with two six-year-olds. And Blue looked sincere. She couldn't blame him entirely for his conduct, knowing his upbringing. He had been no more than a field hand to his grandparents, or so she'd heard.

Cassie settled herself in the comfortable recliner, kicked off her shoes once again, and pushed the chair back. The leg rest anchored her sore feet. She closed her eyes and quickly drifted off to sleep. Images of a dark-haired man with bright blue eyes invaded her dreams.

Two

Cassie was awakened by a finger poking her on the shoulder. Her eyes fluttered open, and she found herself looking into Bree's violet-blue eyes.

"Blue said to tell you dinner is ready," she said to her mother, then slipped her a conspiring look. "Did you know Blue's real name is Neil and that he's half Indian?" Bree didn't wait for a response. "Tara said it was rude to ask him why his skin was darker than ours, but I didn't think so. Do you think it was rude to ask him?"

Cassie blinked, trying to digest everything her daughter had said. She had no idea how to respond to Bree's question, so she changed the subject. "Where is Blue?" she asked, covering a yawn with one slender hand.

"He went to get the hamburgers off the grill."

At the mention of his name, Blue came through

the back door carrying a plate of hamburgers and a spatula. Cassie blushed when his eyes took stock of her long legs on the raised footrest. "Did I sleep long?" she asked, trying to cover her embarrassment. She raised herself from the recliner and stretched, unaware that Blue's eyes were focused on the raw-silk blouse pressing against her breasts.

Blue realized he was staring, but damn, he had never seen such shapely legs! "About an hour," he finally answered, clearing his voice when it sounded unusually hoarse. "You looked like you needed the rest, so I cooked the burgers slow and fed your children junk food." He set the plate of hamburgers on the table and gave her a disarming grin. "I thought you'd appreciate that."

It was difficult not to return the smile. "Very thoughtful of you," she said, coming closer. Instead of slipping on her high heels and enduring more pain, Cassie decided to remain in her stocking feet. Blue seemed to tower over her as a result.

"You'd be surprised how thoughtful I can be when it really counts."

Cassie's stomach fluttered. "I think we're talking about two different subjects."

"Oh? And all this time I thought we understood each other perfectly."

Cassie didn't reply to his sensual banter. It was obvious he enjoyed shaking her up. Instead she took in his neat appearance. He had showered while she napped. His hair was still a bit damp, and he smelled of soap. His slightly worn jeans, which molded to his body, were clean, as was his short-sleeved shirt. Thankfully it was buttoned.

"Are you just going to stand there and stare at me or do you plan to join us for dinner?"

Oh, how smug he could be at times! she thought. "I wasn't staring at you, I was merely surprised to find you had already showered."

"I learned to bathe at an early age despite my heritage," he tossed back. "Now, if you'll have a seat . . ."

"That's not what I meant, Blue," she said with a sigh, disappointed that he thought she was a shallow snob. "I'd like to wash up first, if you don't mind," she said as the girls seated themselves. Cassie saw that Blue had made Tater Tots, a big favorite of her daughters. He had given them each a generous serving. He had even prepared a salad, she noted appreciatively. How could he be so nice one minute and act like such a jerk the next, she wondered.

"The bathroom is down the hall on the left," he told Cassie as he served both girls a sizzling hamburger patty. Tara thanked him and glared at her sister. "You didn't say thank you," she whispered.

"Thank you," Bree said, her mouth already full.

Cassie found the bathroom and washed her face in cold water. Although the brief nap had revived her, she still looked as weary as she felt. Her weariness had more to do with being in Blue's presence, where she was constantly on edge and on guard against her feelings toward him, than with her current situation, she guessed. But she was still faced with the prospect of having nowhere to spend the night. Dusk had settled outside, and she still hadn't made arrangements for a place to stay.

When Cassie took her seat at the table, she noticed the silverware had been set backward. As if reading her thoughts, Blue handed her a hamburger and smiled. "The girls set the table while I cooked." Cassie nodded her understanding.

"I didn't know men could cook," Bree said.

"Not with your mouth full, honey," Cassie told her.

Bree chewed and swallowed. "My daddy doesn't know how to cook."

"Probably because he has never had to learn," Blue said, reaching across to ruffle her hair.

"Do you have any children?" Bree asked, making Cassie squirm in her chair. She was certain Blue had fathered children all over town.

Blue shook his head. "No kids, Curly Locks. Just Duke and me. And some horses and cattle. What about you? You got any kids?"

Bree giggled. "Of course not, silly. I'm only six years old."

He affected a look of surprise. "And all this time I thought you were almost grown-up."

"Is he just teasing, Mommy?" Tara asked when Bree fell into a fit of giggles.

Cassie nodded and shot Blue a derisive smile. "Yes, I'm afraid Mr. Mitchum is just one big tease." She sipped her iced tea and met his gaze over the rim of her glass. She wondered if she would ever be able to look into those blue eyes without her heart skipping a beat. "When I was growing up, he used to tease all the girls in town."

"Except your mommy," Blue said, giving the girls a conspiratorial look. "She never was one for teasing."

Cassie gave him a blank look, hoping nobody at the table knew that his comment had sent her pulse racing. "That's because I'm allergic to penicillin," she said sweetly. Blue threw his head back and laughed. The deep, rich sound of his laughter sent tingles along Cassie's spine.

Both girls looked confused. Bree spoke. "Mommy, what is pen-cil-n?"

"It's too complicated to explain now, Bree," Cassie answered. "You'd better finish your dinner before it gets cold." She felt Blue's amused gaze on her, and it was all she could do to force down her own meal.

"Mr. Mitchum, what kind of pony is that in your barn?" Tara asked.

"Why don't you just call me Blue?" he suggested. "That pony you saw is called a Shetland. Most of them are real high-strung, but not Pippin. He's as gentle as a kitten."

"That's a funny name," Bree said.

"I didn't name him that. I bought him from a couple who moved to Texas. The pony belonged to their daughter."

"I'll bet the little girl was sad," Tara said. "What are you going to do with him?"

He shrugged. "Oh, I plan to stud him—" Blue swallowed the rest of his words as he glanced at Cassie. "Uh, I plan to find him a wife . . . and hopefully they'll start a family just like my cattle do."

"How *do* you make ponies and babies?" Bree asked, looking very serious. Cassie's and Blue's heads turned uneasily in her direction.

"You pray, silly," Tara said, popping a Tater Tot into her mouth. "Isn't that right, Mr. . . . uh, Blue?"

The question caught him off-guard. Nevertheless, he put his elbows on the table and clasped his hands together as though pondering it carefully. "I've heard tell that's one way," he said, the corners of his mouth twitching. "If that doesn't work, I'm sure there's some kind of backup system."

Cassie almost choked on her food. The last thing her daughters needed from Blue Mitchum was a lecture on the act of coupling. Not that the man didn't have it down to an art, she told herself. He probably had notches in his bedpost.

"I promised the girls I'd buy them a pony once we got settled," Cassie announced, trying to change the subject.

"Maybe I can help," Blue offered. "I know a lot of horse breeders—"

"That won't be necessary," she said politely. "I know quite a bit about good horseflesh myself. I used to ride as a child, if you remember. In fact, I must've collected a dozen blue ribbons in riding events," she told the girls proudly. "Of course, you'll have to take riding lessons first."

Blue didn't respond. It was obvious Cassie didn't want or need any suggestions from him. Perhaps she didn't trust his judgment. For some reason it bothered him. But riding lessons, for Pete's sake? What was there to learn? You got on a horse and rode. If you fell off, you just climbed back on. He could teach the girls how to ride in fifteen minutes, but he wasn't about to offer. Suddenly he noticed Bree nodding off over her plate. "I think we have one sleepy little girl on our hands," he said.

"Oh, both girls are probably exhausted," Cassie said, glancing at her wristwatch.

"Cassie, sleep here tonight," Blue prodded gently, feeling sympathetic for the entire group. The feeling was new to him, and it must have been obvious, because Cassie looked as though she might fall out of her chair. "There's plenty of room upstairs. It's not the Hyatt, but you'll be comfortable." He winked. "Besides, your luggage is already here. What more could you ask for?"

Cassie instinctively began to resist, but looking at her tired girls softened the firm set of her lips. Besides, what was her alternative? she asked herself. She had no transportation, no place to stay, and she herself was ready to drop. Tomorrow she would ask Blue to drive her and the girls to the next town, where they could find a motel. Still, it was going to be uncomfortable staying in Blue's house.

"But you've already done so much," she said, feeling herself succumb to the idea of sleeping under his roof. She only hoped she wasn't making a big mistake.

"That's what neighbors are for, fancy britches. Now, why don't we stop arguing, and I'll carry that mountain of luggage upstairs for you. Have you ever thought of hiring a full-time bellboy?"

Cassie stood, resigned to her decision to stay.

Instinct told her she could trust Blue. "I'll clean the kitchen while you're doing that," she said quickly, wanting to make herself useful. "Bree, you go over and lie on the couch until I can get you tucked into bed." The girl nodded, trudged across the room, and fell on the sofa.

Tara jumped up to help her mother. They worked quickly while Blue unloaded their luggage.

"I don't know what I'd do without you," Cassie told Tara, touching her cheek. While Bree was carefree and generous with her affection, Tara was subdued and sensitive beyond her years. It was difficult at times for Cassie to remember she was only six years old.

"Mommy, do you like Mr. Mitchum . . . I mean, Blue?" she asked while Blue was still carrying luggage upstairs.

She was very perceptive, too, Cassie thought, adding to Tara's list of qualities. "Of course I do," she said lightly. "Don't you?"

The little girl shrugged. "He's okay, but I wouldn't want you to marry him."

Cassie's mouth fell open. "Whatever gave you that idea? I haven't laid eyes on the man in years. The only reason we're staying here is that we have no other place to go at the moment. Tomorrow we'll find a place."

Tara looked relieved. "It's just the way he looks at you. I don't want you ever getting married again," she said with conviction. "I didn't like it when you and Daddy were married. You cried a lot. You didn't think I saw, but I did. And you didn't play with us as much. Things got better when Daddy moved out."

Cassie didn't know quite how to respond. Tara had seen through the facade of her and Jean-François's marriage all along. How disturbing it must've been for her to realize her parents merely tolerated one another. "I never knew you felt that way, honey," Cassie said, pulling her daughter close. "From now on, it's just the three of us, okay? We're a team." Tara smiled in response.

"All finished, ladies," Blue said, coming into the room. "I even turned down the covers on the beds." He looked directly at Cassie. "Your bed is right across the hall from where the girls will sleep." He glanced at Bree, who was snoring gently on the couch. "Want me to carry her up?"

"I would appreciate it," Cassie said. "Either they've grown up on me, or my back isn't what it used to be."

Blue lifted Bree easily from the couch and made his way down the hall and up the stairs, with Cassie and Tara in tow. He carried her into a bedroom and laid her on a twin bed, careful not to wake her.

"Thank you," Cassie whispered, already taking off the girl's shoes and socks. Blue nodded, and a second later Cassie heard him descending the stairs. Once she had the sleeping girl bare to her panties, she reached among the suitcases for those that bore Bree's initials. Luckily, she found them without too much trouble. By the time she had finished slipping a fresh gown on Bree, Tara had located her own suitcases. Cassie fished out a rose-colored gown with white tulips stitched along the collar. She handed it to Tara.

"You can skip your bath tonight," Cassie said. "Just be sure to brush your teeth." Tara nodded and disappeared into the bathroom with her toothbrush and toothpaste.

Once the girls were tucked in, Cassie leaned forward and kissed them both. "Good night, honey," she whispered to Tara.

"Where are you going?" the girl asked anxiously.

"To finish cleaning the kitchen."

"Don't stay long."

"I won't. And if you need me tonight, I'll be right across the hall." Tara nodded and turned on her side.

Cassie left the door partially open and stood at the top of the stairs for several seconds. She'd had no idea her daughter felt so possessive of her, but then, that was the way Tara was. "You're going to have to watch that one," their nanny used to say. "She might be quiet, but that doesn't mean she don't have a handful on her mind." Cassie was beginning to understand. While Bree sputtered out her every thought, Tara would carry something inside for months before letting go of it. No doubt the unhappy marriage, the nasty divorce, and Cassie's own state of mind at the time had taken its toll on all of them.

Vowing to make up to her daughters for past hurts, Cassie returned to the kitchen. Blue had already finished cleaning, had made coffee, and was pouring it into two mugs. "Now, why did you finish the cleaning? I came down to do it."

"Because you look like you're about to fall on your face from exhaustion," he said. "Go make yourself comfortable while I sweep the floor." He handed her a mug. "The cream and sugar are on the table."

"No, I like it black," she said, taking it. "I gave up cream and sugar and about a million other goodies when people began stuffing me into tight clothes."

"Maybe you'll be able to enjoy them once again, now that you're back home," he said, beginning to sweep. "You're too thin anyway."

"Thanks, Blue," Cassie said softly and sincerely.

He looked up in surprise. "For what?"

"For everything. For letting us sleep here."

He shrugged. "Did you think I'd just toss you out in the street, for Pete's sake? I may not be a saint, but I'm not completely heartless."

"You've changed."

"Everybody changes. That's what life is about." He reached for the dustpan and swept the litter inside.

"What changed you?"

Blue looked up in surprise. "I've grown up, Cassie," he said matter-of-factly. "Just as you have." His gaze lingered on her lips and dropped to her breasts as if to back up his assertion. A slow smile spread across his face, and his eyes darkened perceptively. "In some ways, though, I'm still the same."

"Meaning?"

"When I see something I want, I go for it."

"And do you always get it?"

His gaze met hers and locked. "Always."

Cassie's heart skipped a beat as his meaning sank in. She had to get away from those fathomless eyes, or she feared she'd drown in them. She excused herself and hurried down the hall. She pushed open the screen door leading to the front porch. Her hands trembled as she held her mug tightly. Once again she had let herself go too far with Blue verbally. One minute their conversation was completely innocent, and the next Blue seemed to be seducing her with words. Perhaps it was her fault for drawing him into conversation after conversation that somehow seemed to turn on her without warning into a sensual play on words. Blue had probably mastered the skill by now. She would certainly have to keep on her toes. The safest thing to do would be to finish her coffee and go straight to bed.

Even though the night was warm, the fans on the ceiling of the porch made it comfortably cool. Cassie spotted the porch swing, walked over, and sank onto it. Energy seemed to seep out of every pore in her body. The bathtub upstairs had looked enticing. Perhaps a good milk bath was what she needed, she thought. She sighed heavily. In her excitement to move back home, she hadn't expected to encounter so many pitfalls. Most of all, she hadn't planned on relying on a man again—especially the notorious Blue Mitchum.

The screen door creaked open and Cassie looked up to find Blue standing in the doorway, holding his cup of coffee. His shoulders spanned the doorframe, and he had to duck slightly as he walked through it. "Mind if I join you?" he asked.

"Please do," Cassie said politely. Despite the fact the man had the ability to shake her up and turn her inside out, he had literally rescued her and her young daughters from an unimaginable plight. Not only that, he was proving to be a perfect host, despite the sensual overtones in everything he said. Perhaps it was just ingrained in his personality. Cassie decided it was time to stop treating him like the enemy, but her conviction faltered when Blue passed the rockers and joined her on the swing.

He sensed her uneasiness. "You can't trust those rockers," he said. "They came with the house, and I haven't had time to repair them. The swing is new." When she continued to look uncomfortable, Blue chuckled deep in his throat. "It's okay, Cassie. I've never forced myself on a woman."

She swallowed a sip of coffee. "But then, you never had to, did you?" she said, trying to sound light and breezy.

"This is my favorite part of the day," Blue said, ignoring her question. His voice was low and seductive and made the hair on the back of Cassie's neck stand up. "Time to put all your thoughts and problems aside and let the frogs and crickets soothe your tired soul."

"Huh?" Cassie was more confused than ever. The Blue Mitchum she had known so long ago wouldn't have had the capacity for such thoughts. He'd been fast and tough and brazen as hell. She could imagine him driving a Harley Davidson and living in a one-room shanty with a tattooed woman, but it was next to impossible to envision him relating to children and kittens and ponies, and living in a respectable farmhouse. Had the world turned upside down?

"Your girls are beautiful," Blue said, and chuckled softly. The sound sent tiny electrical currents up Cassie's back. "I would never have imagined you with twins. You must be very proud of them," he added.

Cassie gave an inaudible sigh of relief. At least they were on a safe topic. "They mean everything to me."

"Won't their father object to your living so far away?" Blue asked. "It won't make visiting them easy."

"He won't object," Cassie said, being deliberately vague. She wasn't about to confess that Jean-François could care less about the girls. Actually, he'd resented them from the beginning. It had nothing to do with the girls; it was simply that Cassie had disobeyed him when she had refused to terminate the pregnancy at the height of her career.

Cassie sucked her breath in sharply as Blue jolted her back to the present by laying his arm against the back of the swing. She stiffened, then realized she was being ridiculous. The man was only trying to make himself comfortable. Lighten up, she told herself.

"So what will you do now?" he asked.

Cassie didn't hesitate. "Build a new life. Start over." She laughed to herself. "And figure out what to do with that miserable thing down the road called a house."

"So you're giving up your career?"

"I didn't say that."

"Is it a topic you'd rather not discuss?"

She shot him a sidelong glance. The moonlight did him justice, silhouetting a perfect set of features. His nose was straight, his jaw square, and his mouth sensual. He was still devastatingly handsome, and he hadn't lost the magnetic pull that had attracted so many women. Why hadn't he married? "Can you keep a secret?" she asked, one corner of her lip turning upward into a smile.

"I've been known to."

This time Cassie laughed out loud. "I'll bet." When he gave her a blank look, she went on. "You mean you never bragged to the guys in the locker room about your conquests with girls?" He looked surprised by her question. "Good grief, you had a waiting line all the way to the Dairy Queen. You should've had your old station wagon bronzed."

Blue was amused. "You're asking me if I was the type to kiss and tell?"

Several fingers trailed across her shoulders as he spoke, and Cassie shivered. Darn the man for possessing such a powerful touch!

"Why don't you try me?" he suggested.

Cassie sat frozen to her spot. Except for the tingling sensations along her spine, her body was in shock. Had Blue just offered to kiss her? Wasn't it bad enough that she had to share the stars with him and inhale his scent? Did he have to tempt her with images of him holding her in those strong arms as well? She wasn't thinking straight. She was tired. Yes, that was it. Otherwise, she would have already leapt from the swing and bounded upstairs as though her life depended on it. She certainly had no business stargazing with Blue Mitchum.

"It has been a long time, hasn't it, Cassie?"

Cassie was startled from her thoughts. "What?"

"Since you've been with a man."

Cassie hoped he didn't see the blush on her face or realize he had touched on the truth. Her marriage had been an empty experience, both physically and emotionally. But Blue didn't have to know. "My personal life isn't open for discussion," she said, staring out into the night.

"I saw it in your eyes the moment I looked at you today," he said, paying no heed to her comment. "The emptiness, the loneliness, the yearning."

"And I suppose you think you're just the man to satisfy all those needs?" She turned toward him abruptly, determined to set him straight. Blue Mitchum hadn't changed as much as she had thought.

"Perhaps."

"When hell freezes over." She made a move to get up and he stopped her by grasping her wrist tightly in his big hand.

"Bitterness doesn't become you, Cassie." Blue released her, took her coffee cup and his, and placed them on the porch rail. With one finger crooked beneath her chin, he raised her face so that she was looking directly into his eyes. "Your

eyes have always been one of your best features
. . . don't let them harden on me."

Cassie realized she had stopped breathing. She
had suddenly become more sensitized to her surroundings. The stars looked like diamond chips
in the sky. Night sounds echoed in her head. A
slight breeze swept across the porch but did very
little to cool her heated flesh. She shivered. Blue's
scent, his warm breath on her cheek, were as
sensual as his lulling baritone voice. His blue eyes
seemed to penetrate right into her soul.

"Know what I think?" he whispered. "I think
you want me to kiss you just as badly as I want
to." Cassie started to object, but before she could
utter a sound, Blue pulled her into his arms and
silenced her with his lips.

Cassie sat motionless, shocked and dazed as
Blue's mouth meshed with hers. Time stood still,
but her frantic heartbeat measured the seconds.
Blue tasted wonderful. Hot and masculine, with a
hint of the coffee he'd just drunk.

Cassie found herself leaning into the kiss as his
arms came around her tighter. She wanted to
absorb the heat from his body, feel the strength of
each muscle and tendon. His chest was pressed
hard against her breasts, and they ached in response. When Blue took them in his hands, she
felt as though a prayer she'd said long ago had
been answered. She hesitantly slipped her arms
around his neck and drew him closer. The kiss
deepened. Blue's tongue slipped past her lips and
explored the depths beyond. Cassie thought she
would literally melt and slide out of the swing as

his tongue made gentle thrusts into her mouth, sending a warm liquid feeling low into her belly. She had no idea what she was doing; she was not thinking, she was *feeling*. She wanted to cry out her disappointment when Blue broke the kiss. They both gasped for air.

For a brief heart-stopping moment, all they could do was stare at each other. Suddenly Blue smiled, and Cassie knew she was lost to his charms. "Does that answer your question?"

She hadn't the slightest idea what he was talking about. The brain cells in her head had clogged and blocked coherent thought. "You mean about the kiss-and-tell part?" she asked dumbly.

Blue laughed. "No, the page you once wrote in your diary about what it would be like to be kissed by me."

Cassie didn't think she had heard him right. "What are you talking about, and what has my diary got to do with anything?" Lord, she'd forgotten all about her diary. At one time she had used it as an outlet to bare her most secret desires. But how could Blue possibly know about her diary?

"I shouldn't tell you," he said.

Cassie crossed her arms and raised her chin stubbornly. "Oh, yes, you will. What about my diary?"

He sighed. She wasn't going to appreciate what he was about to tell her. "Remember the summer your parents hired me to paint the inside of their house?" After a few seconds she nodded. "I think you were fifteen at the time. Well—" He hesitated.

"Well what?" She felt a sinking sensation in her stomach.

"When I got around to painting your room and moving all your furniture around, the drawer to your nightstand fell out, and there it was."

"My diary?"

"Right. It was tempting as hell."

"But I always hid the key."

Blue grinned. "I've broken into tougher things than a diary."

"I'm sure you have," she muttered. "So what did you read?"

"As much as I could."

Cassie blushed to the roots of her hair. "That's terrible!" she said, trying to move as far away from him as she could. "Don't you have any respect for a person's privacy?" He pulled her back into his arms, despite her protests.

"I had less scruples then. I wanted to know what made you so different from the rest of the girls. What made you stick out. Other than being the best-looking girl in town," he added.

Cassie couldn't help feeling a bit flattered at the remark. Coming from the stud of Peculiar, Mississippi, it was quite a compliment. Still, the thought that he had read her innermost secrets, many of which had centered around him, was a bit unnerving. The boys in Peculiar had seemed dull and insignificant compared to Blue. But surely she couldn't have written too many brazen things in a diary she'd received on her fourteenth birthday. "I was just a kid then," she finally said, as if that were explanation enough. "You were older, and such a rebel. I guess I was . . . infatuated. And I had never been kissed," she confessed.

"You should be kissed often."

Cassie decided she didn't like the direction in which the conversation was heading. "I think I'd better go in," she said, deciding it was time to bring the tête-à-tête to a close. She pushed herself up from the swing. This time Blue didn't stop her.

He stood as well. "I never should have told you about the diary." Once more, he was holding her, one hand caressing the small of her back, drawing circles that made her body react in ways she'd never dreamed of.

She shrugged, trying in earnest to sound indifferent, although she wished desperately she could remember exactly what she'd written. No doubt the diary was packed among her things and stored in her parents' attic. She'd find it one day. "It really doesn't matter," she insisted. "As I said, I was only a kid. Kids sometimes fantasize."

"So do adults."

"Please don't do that."

"What?"

"Rub my back like that."

"It feels good, doesn't it? Does it feel *too* good, Cassie?"

Her name sounded like a velvet whisper on his lips. Cassie pretended not to hear him as she pulled free, picked up their coffee cups, and carried them into the house. She suddenly realized she was trembling from head to toe. Blue Mitchum had not just kissed her, he had kissed her thoroughly. Damn thoroughly. He followed her into the kitchen, waited until she set the cups in the sink, then reached for her again.

"I could gobble you up," he said.

"Blue—" Cassie didn't doubt it for a moment. His eyes were filled with desire. "This isn't going to work if I have to run from you."

"You're running in circles, you know. If I wanted to, I'd take you without a second thought."

"What's stopping you, then?" she said defiantly, tired of his underlying threats, which he'd subtly been tossing at her all evening.

"Because I'm a patient man. I'm willing to wait for you to come to me."

The grin on his face made her wonder if he was serious. "Me come to you? That'll be the day, Blue Mitchum."

"Just answer one question. Was the kiss what you expected?"

She knew she ought to lie, but it was impossible to look into those stark blue eyes and not be honest. "Yes, it was good," she confessed in a whisper-soft voice. "Better than I expected. That's why it's never going to happen again."

Blue gave her a knowing smile. "Never say never. As I said, you need to be kissed often. And then, when you're ready, I'm going to take you to the moon."

"Only in your dreams," she tried to say in a forceful tone as she walked on wobbly legs down the hall and up the stairs under Blue's watchful gaze. As she gave him one last glance over her shoulder, she felt her stomach flutter as though a hummingbird had somehow become trapped inside.

"Good night, Cassie," he said gently.

Cassie mumbled a reply from the top of the stairs and hurried into the bedroom opposite her daughters'. She sank onto a plump feather mattress and closed her eyes. She had made a mistake thinking she could stay in Blue Mitchum's house.

She would leave first thing in the morning.

Three

When Cassie opened her eyes the next morning, she found her legs were tangled with a pair of short skinny ones. She moved the covers about, and discovered Tara sleeping beside her. She must've become frightened in the night, Cassie thought. The house was quiet. Perhaps Bree was sleeping late as well. After having spent the previous day traveling from one end of the country to the other, hurrying across airports and trying to make connections, it was no wonder they were all exhausted.

Cassie finally sat up, her yearning for coffee outweighing her desire for more sleep. Actually, she felt more rested than she had in months. Her old life was over, and her new life was just beginning. Her problems didn't seem as overwhelming with the morning sun slanting through the venetian blinds as they had when she'd climbed into bed the night before. Despite being tired, she had spent a long time thinking about Blue's kiss and trying to put it into perspective. Blue enjoyed flirting with a pretty woman, she told herself, but what he enjoyed more was the chase. The fact that she was unattainable would no doubt rouse his curiosity even more. He had been testing his ground. One slipup was permissible, perhaps expected from a man like Blue Mitchum, but from now on she would keep her distance. She would find a place to stay, no matter what.

Cassie stretched and reached for a matching robe to the gown she wore. It had been given to her by the designer for whom she'd modeled it. The ivory material was of raw silk and felt wonderful against her skin. Cassie stood and checked her reflection in the mirror over an antique bureau. Her eyes looked rested, but her hair was in wild disarray.

Those same violet-blue eyes and wild hair had made her famous.

"Why would you want to design clothes when you should be modeling them?" Jean-François had asked when she confessed her reasons for moving to New York. It was because of Jean-François's insistence that Cassie had agreed to a photo session with a German photographer named Max. When his assistant made an attempt to draw her hair back from her face, Jean-François had adamantly objected.

"*Non, non, non!*" Jean-François had exclaimed to the surprised assistant. "I want Mademoiselle's hair loose and untamed." He beseeched Max, "Look at her eyes. Have you ever seen eyes that color? And that look of innocence. She appears unblemished, *oui*? But that hair makes her look wild and wanton."

Cassie had felt the heat rush to her cheeks. She'd licked her bottom lip nervously. The room had been cold and she'd been braless. She'd felt her nipples contract beneath the flimsy off-the-shoulder evening dress she'd worn. Those same nipples had appeared as tight little buds when Jean-François had delivered the glossies to her several days later.

"The camera loves you! I am going to turn you into the highest-paid model in New York. Of course, you'll have to lose ten pounds right away. The camera has a habit of adding pounds to even the most perfect body."

Jean-François had hired several makeup artists and hairstylists, and in just a few short weeks had created the image he'd sought for Cassie. She hadn't recognized herself. She'd looked wild and untamed and provocative.

But his plan succeeded beyond her wildest imagination. Six months later, Jean-François had kissed her hard on the lips "Say you'll marry me and make my life perfect."

Cassie had been stunned by the proposal—she hadn't even seen it coming. But how could she have denied him? He'd been her best friend, her *only* friend in New York.

They'd married three days later without any pomp or fuss. Cassie had called her parents, who were unable to hide their disappointment that they had never met her new husband and had dreamed of Cassie being married in their church. She hadn't told her parents that her new husband was almost twenty-five years older than she.

"I'm sorry we could not be married with your family present as you wished, darling," Jean-François had said. "But we have a tight schedule ahead of us." He had slipped her a slender velvet box containing a diamond necklace as if to placate her, something he would do over and over again to make amends for not being a good husband. Cassie had hugged him. Surely her husband loved her deeply to give her such a gift, she'd believed.

Now, as Cassie stood staring at her face in the mirror, she realized it had been the beginning of the end. Jean-François had not wanted a flesh-and-blood wife. He'd wanted a procelain statue that made all the right turns and twists, one who could "seduce the camera," as he so often put it. He had fallen in love with the woman in the photos, the woman he'd created. As a wife, Cassie bored him. She found it ironic now that one of his rare visits to her bedroom had produced something worth living for: Bree and Tara. Although she had been generous about granting him access to the girls, she hadn't been surprised that Jean-François had never taken advantage of visitation rights. She had known in her heart he would be too "busy" to visit his daughters. She had done it more for the girls than for him. No matter what, she wanted them to think their father loved them.

Cassie quietly left her room and went into the one where Bree was sleeping. The bed was empty. Perhaps she was watching cartoons, Cassie thought, hurrying down the stairs. But both the kitchen and the den were empty. Panic caused her stomach to flutter wildly as she ran out the back door in her gown and robe. The grass was wet beneath her feet as she circled the house calling her daughter. Where was Blue, she wondered.

Then a thought came to her mind. The new kittens! Bree would be eager to play with them. Cassie hurried toward the barn, coming to a halt in the doorway. The barn was empty except for the animals. She called out for Bree, but there was no answer. Adrenaline shot through Cassie's body, and she ran the full length of the building and out the other side. She caught sight of her daughter and went limp with relief.

"Good morning, sleepyhead," Blue called out.

"Mommy, look," Bree said excitedly. "Blue is giving me a ride on Pippin."

Cassie could feel her heart still pounding as Blue led the Shetland in a wide circle while Bree straddled him bareback and in her nightgown. If she hadn't already been frightened out of her wits, she would have found the sight endearing.

"Shouldn't you have checked with me before running out of the house?" she asked, her voice disapproving. "You had me worried." Bree's eyes widened at her mother's stern tone. Blue stopped leading the pony, and the three of them stared at one another.

Bree was the first to speak. "But Blue said not to wake you up 'cause you were probably real tired."

Blue read the anxiety in Cassie's eyes. He understood it to be a result of her mistrust of him with her children. She was the most overprotective mother he'd ever seen. And it didn't stop there. She was all wired up for some reason. He hadn't seen her relax since she arrived. "I think your mom is ready for you to go inside now," he said. He lifted Bree from the horse and set her on the ground.

For the first time in her life, Bree didn't insist on having her way. "Can I watch cartoons until breakfast?" she asked. When Cassie nodded, the girl scurried through the barn toward the house as though she sensed she would be better off being out of sight.

Blue didn't speak for a moment. He reeled in the rope tied to the Shetland until the pony was beside him. His face was devoid of expression. "Something bothering you, Cassie?"

Cassie suddenly felt ridiculous. She was overreacting and she knew it, but she reacted defensively. "I wake up and find my daughter missing, and you want to know what's bothering me."

"What did you think had happened to her?" he asked, eyeing her steadily.

"How was I supposed to know?"

Blue led the pony back into the barn and into its stall. Once he'd freed the animal from its hal-

ter, he stepped out and closed the door. Cassie
stood rooted just inside the barn door. Blue sucked
his breath in sharply at the sight of her body
silhouetted in the sunlight, her ivory gown and
robe appearing as sheer as gossamer. The curves
of her breasts caught and held his attention until
his gaze wandered to her trim waistline and slightly
flared hips. Her hair was as untamed as the desire that suddenly shot through his loins. When
he spoke, it took every ounce of control to keep
his voice from shaking.

"Let's get down to what's really bothering you,"
he said, wondering how he could sound so calm
with his body so aroused.

"Which is?" Cassie was determined to remain
cool, despite the looks he kept shooting her.

"You don't trust me with your girls."

Cassie didn't know what to say. Still, she didn't
deny it. "I don't know you, Blue," she said matter-
of-factly. "The Blue Mitchum I used to know was
mean and wild and irreverent."

Blue closed the distance between them slowly,
his gaze holding hers as tightly as he'd held the
pony's rope earlier. He stopped only inches from
Cassie. "Let's get a few things straight between
us, *Mrs.* D'Clair," he said in clipped words. "I'm
not going to hurt your little girls or teach them
my wicked ways."

Cassie was taken aback by the hard look he
gave her. "I never accused you of it."

"No, but it crossed your mind, or you wouldn't
have come running out here. You've always run
from me, Cassie. But one of these days you're

going to run to me, and it won't be because I'm with your daughter." He stepped closer. His gaze dropped to her breasts.

"I certainly hope you don't think I would ever—"

"Like I said, never say never," he interrupted. "It has a way of backfiring on you." He reached out to touch the collar on her robe. She stiffened, and he smiled. "Nice material," he said, the pitch of his voice seducing her nervous system. "When you *do* decide to go to bed with me, I'd like you to wear this."

Other than being outright shocked, Cassie was tempted to slap the smug look off his face. "The very idea that I would willingly climb into your bed is preposterous," she said.

Blue chuckled and leaned closer. "Eager women hate themselves for their own desire and would rather place the blame with me. But they're always the hungriest in bed."

Cassie's fists balled at her sides. "I'm leaving," she ground out between clenched teeth. "I refuse to stay here any longer and put up with this . . . this gutter talk."

"Want to borrow the Shetland?" he asked, amusement lurking in his eyes. " 'Course, it's going to take all day to haul that luggage of yours."

She twirled around on her heel and headed for the house. She felt Blue's hand close around her wrist. All at once Cassie found herself immobile. He spun her around and pulled her hard against his chest.

"You're not going anywhere," he said, his voice authoritative. He glanced down at her shocked face and parted lips, and his mouth captured hers hungrily. At first Cassie tried to push away, but his arms only tightened around her. His tongue was hot as it speared past her lips and explored beyond. One thigh slipped between her legs and pressed against her femininity. Cassie felt the heat of her temper cool while other parts of her body grew hot. The kiss lingered and grew gentle. When Blue finally released her, they stared at each other as if for the first time.

"I'm going to get you in my bed come hell or high water," he said, his voice husky. "But I'd kill the bastard that tried to harm your daughters."

Cassie sighed helplessly. He was so handsome when the sun glinted on that blue-black hair and his eyes darkened with desire. No wonder women were tempted beyond rational thinking. "I can't stay here," she said, changing the subject so quickly, Blue was caught by surprise. "I have to leave immediately."

"You have no choice, Cassie," he said, stroking her cheek. "Besides, there's plenty of room here, and you're close to your house."

"Are you suggesting we move in?" she asked in total disbelief. She took a step back. As long as he wasn't touching her, she could keep her resolve. "Have you forgotten I have two little girls who will be attending first grade here in the fall? I'm not about to let them be the subject of gossip."

Blue pondered the thought. "Okay, I'll hire a housekeeper. You'll need help with the girls anyway when you start work on the house. The housekeeper can act as a part-time nanny. That should stop tongues from wagging." The thought of her leaving bothered him more than he wanted to admit. In less than twenty-four hours, she had managed to turn his world upside down. He wanted her, and he was determined to have her.

Cassie was already shaking her head. "It won't work, Blue."

"We'll make it work. Then in two weeks your folks will be back, and you can move in with them until your house is finished. Why make the drive back and forth from the next town when this is so convenient?"

"The mere thought is ridiculous. And after last night . . . and just now—" She stopped abruptly.

"You don't trust yourself?" he drawled.

"You're so smug."

"Not smug, just confident. Besides, I already told you. I'm going to wait for *you* to come to *me*. That's what this is all about, fancy pants. I want you to come to me as Cassie Kennard, not some highfalutin celebrity who thinks she's too good for me." He stepped closer, and when he spoke, his voice was little more than a whisper. "Who knows? You might like sleeping with a savage. It excites some women."

"You're disgusting."

"And you're a tease."

Cassie's mouth dropped open. Of all things, she'd never been accused of being a tease. "That's not true," she said, her voice trembling with indignation.

"Oh, yeah? Then why did you turn liquid in my arms last night, and why are you wearing that sexy gown?" Cassie crossed her arms over her breasts. "When I respond, as any red-blooded man would, you back off as if I've got the plague. I don't think it's me you're worried about, Miss High-and-Mighty. I think you're worried about what *you* might do. You'd die before you let anyone in this town think you were sleeping with me."

Cassie, who had remained quiet throughout his lecture, didn't know what to say. But she refused to let somebody like Blue Mitchum make such accusations. He was testing her, perhaps trying to intimidate her. She would show him. After what she'd been through with Jean-François, she wasn't frightened by any man.

"Okay, I'll stay," she said, noting the look of surprise on his face. "But I'll interview potential housekeepers, and if I find someone I like, I'll pay her salary. If she's good, I'll take her with me when I leave. Not only that, I'll pay rent. And once my parents return, we'll be out of here." It all sounded cold and businesslike, but she preferred it that way.

He gave her a hard look. "I refuse to charge you rent."

"Then I'll buy the groceries." When he looked as though he might argue, her expression remained firm. He finally shrugged his shoulders as though it weren't worth worrying about. "When does the weekly paper come out?" she asked.

"Tomorrow. I know a couple of girls who work in the classified department. I'll see if I can slip an ad in the help-wanted section right away." He talked as though the problem had already been taken care of.

Cassie couldn't help frowning. Blue Mitchum probably had clout with just about every female in town. "I would appreciate it. The sooner, the better." She paused. "Why are you grinning like that?"

"Because you're a hypocrite."

"My, but you've managed to cover all of my finer qualities this morning," she said sarcastically. "Are there any more flaws in my personality you'd like to point out?"

He grinned. "I'll have to see what you're like in bed first."

Cassie decided not to respond. To do so would merely keep the argument alive. Instead, she turned abruptly and headed for the house. Why she had ever agreed to stay was beyond her. She tried to list the reasons as she walked: because she had no place else to stay; because it was so convenient to her house; because she didn't have a car. But the fact that she was attracted to Blue had nothing to do with it, she told herself. She would keep her distance. Having a housekeeper around would cool his ardor. Even a man like Blue, despite his lack of scruples, would back off with a complete stranger in the house. In the meantime, she'd stick close to her girls. Blue couldn't very well seduce her in front of a couple of six-year-olds. She smiled at the thought.

Blue leaned against the barn and watched Cassie make her way toward the house, looking as though she were enveloped in a silk cloud. Damn, she was tempting. But then, she'd been a tempting little morsel all her life. He had wanted her from the moment she had started to blossom from a skinny kid into a beautiful woman. Then, before he'd had a chance, she'd left town. He frowned. He wouldn't have people gossiping about her. He would place the ad right away. But that didn't mean he would stop pursuing her.

The next day, Cassie followed two middle-aged men through the house she'd bought, impatiently waiting for some word from them. Bart and Dirk Suthers owned a carpentry business. Cassie had called them the day before, despite Blue's look of disapproval.

"Well, what do you think?" she asked once they had inspected the house thoroughly. "Can the place be salvaged?"

"Depends," Dirk answered, "on how much money you're plannin' to spend, and how much time you got. We're almost finished with another job. I 'spect we could start on this place in a couple of days and be done in three months."

"Three months!" she shrieked. "But you can build a house from the ground up in four!"

"And it's a heck of a lot easier building from scratch than having to tear out and start over," Bart said.

Cassie sighed. That meant she would be living with her parents the entire time. It also meant putting her new career on hold. She couldn't wait; plans and scheduling were already in motion. She had to get to work.

"I don't have three months," she said. "I'll give you a month to get the downstairs livable." At the look of disbelief on their faces, she continued. "There's a bonus in it for you if you meet the deadline. It just means you'll have to work a couple of weekends."

"You'd plan to live here while we work on the upstairs?" Dirk asked, as though he found it impossible to believe. "I mean, it's gonna be kinda noisy with us sawin' and hammerin'—"

"I have twins; I'm accustomed to noise. Besides, that way I'll be able to oversee the work on the house as well as carry on with my own business," she added in what she hoped was a subtle hint that she'd be watching them. "When can you give me an estimate on the costs?" she asked. "I plan to get one or two more quotes before I decide."

Bart scratched his head. "I'll have to go through the place with a calculator. You'll need all new sinks, tubs, and fixtures. I'll have to get a roof man out. Personally, I think you're going to have to replace the whole roof. I'll have to see how well the place is insulated—"

"How long will this take?" Cassie repeated.

"Couple of days."

"Fine. Here's a number where you can reach me. Call me as soon as you have the figures." They left the house and Cassie summoned the girls from the swing that Blue had spent the morning repairing with a new rope. They all piled into Blue's jeep.

Blue had parked the jeep beneath a shade tree and was leaning back with a straw hat covering his face as though he had all the time in the world. He had purposely stayed in the jeep, not wanting to interfere with Cassie's plans for the house. The Suthers brothers weren't his idea of top-notch carpenters, but he'd bite his tongue off before mentioning it to Cassie. She had made it clear she wanted to make her own decisions, and Blue was going to let her do just that.

"What did the Smothers brothers say?" Blue couldn't resist asking.

Cassie frowned at him. "Suthers, not Smothers. They are going to give me an estimate in a couple of days. In the meantime, I'm going to get another quote on the house."

Blue nodded but didn't say anything. When he pulled into his driveway a few minutes later, Duke lumbered out to meet them as usual. "Stay in the jeep," he told Cassie as the girls bolted out of the vehicle and ran in the direction of the barn.

She gave him a blank look. "What for?"

"You got a driver's license?"

"Of course I do. I always keep my license up-to-date for identification purposes. Why?"

"I'm going to teach you how to drive this jeep."

Cassie laughed out loud. "You can't be serious! Do you realize how long it's been since I've driven a car? Not to mention one with a stick shift. I rode a bus in New York until—"

"Until you worked your way up to limos," he said. "Well, you're not in New York anymore, and you're going to have to learn to get around. After you learn to drive, I'll take you to the next town, and you can look for a car."

Cassie wore a grim look. "I don't know, Blue."

Blue climbed out of the jeep and motioned for her to slide over to the driver's seat. He walked around to the passenger side and got in. Then he took a deep breath as though he dreaded the ordeal as much as she. *Somebody* had to teach her, he told himself.

"Okay," Blue said. "Let's go over a few things just to see what you remember." Cassie looked bemused. "You remember where the accelerator and the brakes are?" When she pointed them out, he nodded. "Good. Now, see that other pedal down there next to the brake? That's called a clutch."

"Should I be taking notes?" she asked.

He ignored her. "The clutch is used when you change gears. Now, there are four gears here—"

Cassie listened as he gave her a complete rundown on what each gear was used for. It was difficult to concentrate, with him sitting so close. She caught his scent on the air and completely forgot where third gear was.

"Okay, are you ready to try it?" Blue asked, wiping sweat from his brow. He'd picked a hell of a day to teach her to drive. His blue workshirt clung to him, and he noticed that her lightweight knit blouse was damp between her breasts. It was oddly stimulating to think of those tiny beads of sweat trickling down the valley between those perfect mounds.

"You don't really expect me to drive this thing, do you?" she asked in disbelief.

"Why the hell do you think I've been sitting here in the hot sun going over all this?" Blue demanded, trying to hold his temper—and keep his mind on the lesson and off her body. "Now, what's the first thing you do when you're ready to drive?"

"I turn the key in the ignition."

"Wrong. You step on the clutch."

"But I'm not going to change gears, I'm just going to start the darn thing!" The heat was not helping Cassie's mood.

"Okay, start it."

Cassie turned the key in the ignition. The jeep came to life, lurched forward, and died. Beside her, Blue crossed his arms over his wide chest and looked the other way as if to say, "I told you so." Cassie pressed the clutch to the floor and turned the ignition once more. The motor churned. "Okay, now what?"

"You want to go in reverse," Blue told her.

Cassie struggled with the stick shift until she finally found reverse. She stepped on the gas and the jeep shot out of the driveway, sailed across the street, and came close to running into a ditch.

"Step on the brake!" Blue bellowed beside her.

Cassie slammed on the brakes, and Blue's head collided with the windshield. "Good Lord, are you trying to kill us?" he yelled.

"You told me to step on the brake," she shouted back.

"I didn't expect you to throw your whole body into it."

Cassie gritted her teeth. For the next half-hour she practiced changing gears until Blue felt she could back out onto the road. She drove less than five hundred feet from the house before he told her to turn around and head back. When she parked the jeep in the driveway, neither was speaking. Cassie climbed out, slammed the door, and marched away.

"Tomorrow we'll practice early," Blue called out. "When it's not so hot." Although Cassie ignored him, Blue fastened his gaze on her tempting fanny as she stalked toward the house. Her hair had come loose from the ribbon she'd tied around it, and Blue couldn't help but wonder what she'd look like naked with that wild hair hanging down around her shoulders.

Blue entered the house and went straight to the small room at the back that he used as an office. He checked his answering machine, on which were several messages for him and one message for Cassie. He scribbled down the telephone number and left his office. He found her in the kitchen sipping a glass of iced tea. "You had a call from a lady at the *Messenger*," he said.

Cassie looked up in surprise. "The newspaper? What does she want?"

"She wants to do an interview. Famous-model-comes-home stuff, I reckon."

"I wonder how they found out so quickly that I was in town?" she said, thinking out loud. Cassie was not the least bit eager to do a newspaper interview, due to the fact that she was temporarily living in Blue Mitchum's house. Once the readers discovered that tidbit, it would cause quite a stir. On the other hand, if she refused to do the interview, it might look as though she were trying to hide something. She should have anticipated that something like this would happen.

"I don't know what to do," Cassie confessed.

"Well, don't ask me," Blue grumbled. "You've turned down every offer I've made."

Cassie tried to push his remark aside, but there was an element of truth to what he'd said. She still hadn't forgotten the old Blue Mitchum—hell-raiser, fighter, and womanizer. "As I said, Blue, you may have changed, but you'll have to give me time to adjust."

As she spoke, Blue noticed that the strands in her hair were a variety of browns and golds. Her eyes were dark, more violet than blue. He'd always been baffled by the color of her eyes. Her lips were full, and even without lipstick they were a light peach color. How he'd like to take that bottom lip between his teeth. If she knew half the things he had thought of doing to her, she would have packed her bags and left, even if it meant staying in the next town.

"Cassie, do you trust me?" Blue asked curiously, knowing it was an ironic thing to ask after the thoughts he'd just entertained about making love to her.

"I suppose so. Why?"

"But not entirely?"

Her look was unwavering. "I once gave a man my unconditional trust. He almost destroyed me. I will never let another human being have that much power over me again."

Blue would have had to be deaf not to catch the bitterness in her voice. He wanted to pull her into his arms and reassure her. "Not all men are like that, Cassie." He paused and studied the features that could be so lovely one moment and so distant the next.

"I'm not taking any more chances," she said matter-of-factly.

Blue shook his head, his look grim. "That French bastard really did a number on you, didn't he?"

Four

Two days later, Cassie paced the floor, waiting for
the doorbell to ring. The fact that her palms were
damp surprised her. She had been interviewed
for *Vogue*, *Cosmopolitan*, and *Harper's Bazaar*,
to name just a few, so why was she so worked up
over a simple interview for her hometown newspaper? Because she knew these people, she told
herself. She had grown up in this town. Now her
friends had children of their own, and it was very
important to Cassie that they approve of her, at
least for the sake of her daughters. She had a
terrible, overwhelming dread of Bree and Tara
being ostracized because of their mother's chosen
career and the nasty publicity that had followed
her divorce.

"Mommy, how much longer do we have to sit
here?" Bree asked.

"The reporter should be here any minute," Cassie assured both girls. They were dressed in crisp pink pinafores and wore matching bows in their fine blond hair, which tended to be as unruly as their mother's. Cassie, not wanting to flaunt her success, wore a stylish blue cotton chambray skirt and blouse with sandals. She had pulled her hair up into a demure bun, but already it was threatening to come loose.

The doorbell rang and Cassie's heart fluttered for several seconds before she regained her composure. When she opened the door, the smile on her face drooped in disappointment. Jenny Bowers, who was no more than a gossip columnist, stood on the front porch. Anxiety surged through Cassie's veins, but she'd die before she'd let it show.

"Miss Bowers, come in," Cassie said, holding the door open. She regained her composure immediately. "How nice to see you again after all these years." The women shook hands. Jenny's smile looked as fake as the one Cassie had plastered on her own lips.

"Thank you for granting the interview," Jenny said. She introduced the photographer, and the three went into the den. "Oh, how sweet your girls look," Jenny exclaimed with a smile once she saw Tara and Bree, both of whom writhed and squirmed on the sofa like a couple of worms in a bucket.

"Thank you." Cassie motioned to a chair. "Won't you have a seat?" Cassie took her place beside the girls on the couch. The photographer stood off to the side, making adjustments to his camera. "Would you like something to drink?" Cassie asked. "I have coffee or lemonade." Both declined her offer, which was fine with Cassie. She had never cared for Jenny Bowers anyway. Jenny had hung out with some of Blue's crowd at one point and had had the reputation of being fast. She was one of several girls who'd worn too much makeup and in whose wake trouble seemed to follow. That was a long time ago, Cassie told herself. What bothered her now was the fact that they'd sent Jenny to do the interview in the first place. In the past, Cassie had always been interviewed by top editors, *selected* professionals in their fields.

"So," Jenny said, breaking into Cassie's thoughts, "how does it feel to be home again after living a posh existence in New York?"

The question didn't surprise Cassie; in fact, she had expected as much. She gave the woman a glowing smile. "I'm thrilled to be home," she said. "And my life in New York was not as exciting as some may think. Anyone who knows the rigors of modeling will agree," she added. "I worked very hard."

"Hmm." Jenny tapped her pencil against her notebook. "And it all looks so easy, just sitting there doing nothing."

Cassie decided not to dignify the remark with an answer. If Jenny was going to be a snit, Cassie would make her work for the interview. As though sensing Cassie's changing mood, Jenny became all smiles.

"So tell me, Cassie. What made you decide to

run off to New York and become a high-fashion model?"

Cassie saw her girls yawning and hoped they wouldn't be needed long. "I hadn't intended on becoming a model when I went to New York," she said. "I studied fashion and design for two years after high school, and I had originally planned to go into designing." In the background, Cassie could hear the photographer snapping pictures. She gave a self-conscious laugh. "In the process, I ended up on the other side of the camera." She wasn't about to confess that it had been at Jean-François's insistence.

"Tough break, huh?" Jenny said, a hint of sarcasm in her voice. She had the good sense to act as though she were teasing, but Cassie knew better. "So what are your plans now?" the woman asked.

"I'm having the old Kelsey house renovated and am waiting for my parents to return from a camping trip."

Jenny nodded. "I understand you're living here in Mayor Mitchum's house in the meantime," she said, taking in her surroundings. "Do you think it'll hurt his chances for reelection?"

Cassie's face went blank. "I beg your pardon?"

Jenny obviously didn't see the shocked expression on Cassie's face as she scribbled on her pad. "Do you think the gossip circulating around town about the two of you will hinder Mayor Mitchum's chances, should he choose to run for another term?"

Cassie was ready to answer the question, when

Blue slammed through the back door. "Damn, it's hot out there!" He took in the scene before him, and he winced. "Looks like I came in at a bad time," he said apologetically.

Cassie was mortified. Jenny let out a soft gasp. Not only had Blue discarded his shirt, but his worn denims, which rode low on his hips, were molded to every sensual line of his thighs. He'd tied a red bandanna around his forehead, which was soaked with perspiration, and his heavily matted chest wore a sheen of sweat. He was maleness in its rawest form.

The twins jumped up from their place beside Cassie and ran to him. "Are you finished working for the day?" Bree asked excitedly.

"Will you take us for a ride on Pippin?" Tara asked a bit shyly, still keeping her distance.

Jenny Bowers spoke. "My, but this *is* a cozy group we have here. If I didn't know better, I'd think you were the Brady Bunch."

"Mayor Mitchum has been very kind," Cassie said, trying not to choke on her words. "And he's wonderful with the girls." She smiled at Blue, but her words were meant for Jenny. "I know the mayor will be glad to be rid of us," she added. "I'm sure we're in his way." Snake in the grass, she thought, glaring at Blue. Why hadn't he told her that he was the mayor of Peculiar? She barely caught the frown on Blue's face before she turned back to Jenny, who seemed confused.

Jenny directed her attention to Blue. "Mr. Mayor, as I was telling Mrs. D'Clair, there has been some gossip about the two of you living under the same roof."

Blue shrugged. "Mrs. D'Clair and her girls are using my upstairs until her parents return. So what?" It was obvious Blue wasn't the least bit intimidated by Jenny's insinuations.

She gave him a patronizing smile. "Well, you know how some of our older citizens are. They might frown on such an arrangement. Some say it might hurt your chances for reelection."

Blue's voice gave away none of the hostility that was brewing inside him. "Miss Bowers, if opening my door to a woman and her two children seems wrong to this community, then I think the citizens of Peculiar should search their own hearts and ask themselves if they wouldn't do the same. I have enough confidence in the people of this town to think they would." He paused in thought. "Come to think of it, I believe there's mention in the Bible about opening your door to others. I can't quote the verse. Perhaps you can get one of the more pious members of the community to locate it."

Jenny seemed at a loss for words. Blue wasn't. "Now, let me show you the way out, Miss Bowers," he offered in a tone that told her she was dismissed. "You, too, cameraman." The photographer, who had remained quiet throughout the interview, followed the two out of the room after Jenny managed to choke out her thanks to Cassie and the girls.

Once they were out the door, Blue caught Jenny by the arm as the photographer headed toward the car. Jenny looked up in surprise. "Let's get something straight, Miss Bowers," Blue said, his eyes as frosty as his tone of voice. "You print anything bad about Mrs. D'Clair, and I'll personally see to it you never write for our newspaper again."

Jenny was clearly taken aback. "My, aren't we being protective?" she said. "Do you treat all your, uh . . . guests with the same courtesy?"

"I am always courteous to those who deserve it. Mrs. D'Clair is a lady, and I refuse to see her treated otherwise."

Jenny gritted her teeth. "What makes you think she's such a lady, Blue? I've seen some of the lingerie ads she has posed for."

"How do I know she's a lady?" Blue asked, as though he hadn't heard a word she'd said. "Because Cassie never once climbed in the back of my station wagon. As I recall, you did. Several times, in fact." He watched the color drain from Jenny's face. "You write a nasty column, and I'll see that you never write for the *Messenger* again."

Jenny's face turned a bright shade of red. "That's blackmail!"

"Damn right it is." Blue closed the door in her face.

When he reentered the house, he found Cassie still glued to her spot on the couch. The girls had gone upstairs to change clothes. He leaned against the doorframe, noting how pretty Cassie looked, despite the grave look on her face.

"You lied to me," she said.

He knew without being told that she was talking about his political office. "I never lied," he responded, coming into the room. "I just didn't want to make a big deal out of it, that's all. Besides, it's *not* a big deal. Not in a town this size. I don't even have an office. I use a room off the kitchen to work."

"So that's why that door is always locked," Cassie mused aloud. She sighed heavily. "I can't stay."

"Let's not go through that again, for heaven's sake. Didn't you say you already had two interviews set up tomorrow for a housekeeper?"

"What if Jenny decides to make a big deal out of it?"

"She won't," Blue assured her.

"How do we *know* that?"

Blue sat down beside her and took one of her slender hands in his. They were beautiful hands, hands made for stroking and caressing. "Trust me, Cassie."

Their gazes met. Cassie was very much aware of Blue's masculinity. Although he had donned his shirt the minute he'd walked in from the heat, it was unbuttoned and exposed his chest. The red headband gave him a wild, uncivilized look that spoke to some untamed region of Cassie's femininity. Blue lifted a finger beneath her jaw and tipped up her face. His lips touched one corner of her mouth, then the other. Cassie didn't move.

He pulled back hesitantly. "I don't want to get you dirty," he said, taking in the liquid violet-blue eyes that never ceased to amaze him. "I'm sure I smell worse than the animals in the barn."

"You always smell nice to me," Cassie said truthfully.

Blue's eyes darkened. "You're treading on dangerous ground, Mrs. D'Clair." They were interrupted by the appearance of the twins.

"Can we ride Pippin now?" Bree asked, jumping up and down.

"*May*," Cassie corrected.

"Yes, you may," Blue said. But the look in his eyes told Cassie he had more interesting things on his mind than giving pony rides. "You'll each get two turns, and then I come in for a shower. Agreed?" Both girls nodded and raced out the door. "What are you going to do?" he asked Cassie.

"Change into something more comfortable. I can't believe I used to spend all my time dressed in uncomfortable clothes. Then I want to call the Suthers brothers to arrange a time to meet them tomorrow." She knew everything she was saying was superficial and that she really wanted to ask Blue to kiss her again, to hold her . . . She dropped her gaze, knowing how perceptive he could be. At times she wondered if he was a mind reader.

"Well, I'd better get to the barn before those two try to saddle the pony without me." He hurried out the back door and across the yard.

Cassie realized she was clasping her hands tightly, and she loosened her grip. Blue hadn't fooled her for one minute. He might pretend indifference to his political office, but she knew that it *had* to mean a lot to him after years of being treated as an outcast. In her heart, she knew he had to feel honored that the town trusted him enough to elect him. She couldn't jeopardize his career.

She and the girls had to get out immediately!

Without hesitating, Cassie stood and hurried up the stairs to change. Once dressed, she began stuffing clothes into the suitcases as fast as she could. Her hands trembled. Once she had everything in order, she began carrying her luggage downstairs. If Blue refused to take her to the next town, she would call the sheriff's office.

"Just what the hell do you think you're doing?"

Cassie jumped as she set the last of her luggage next to the front door. She turned and found herself looking into a pair of ominous blue eyes. "We have to leave, Blue," she said simply. "I refuse to stay here and risk ruining your political career, not to mention what it might do to the girls. Where are they?" She glanced around him anxiously.

"In the barn playing with the kittens." He didn't sound friendly. "It seems they feel more comfortable here than their mother, but then, of course, they're too young to worry about idle gossip." He folded his arms over his chest. "You disappoint me, Cassie."

"Don't start on me, Blue. You know I'm doing what's best."

"Oh? And what are the girls supposed to do, sit in a motel room all day? They're having a ball here, and I suspect after what they've been through they need some fun in their lives."

Cassie felt as though he'd just slapped her. "I have tried to prevent them from getting hurt."

"So what's the use of hiring a housekeeper if you're leaving?" he asked. "Perhaps you would feel better if I hired a full-time security guard to protect you in case I turn into a wild Indian."

"That's not funny."

"Neither is this," he said, motioning to the luggage. "Your parents are going to be back in eight days."

"A lot can happen in that length of time, Blue." Cassie saw the look of surprise on his face and regretted her words instantly.

"For example?"

She raised her chin. "I don't think I have to spell it out for you. We're both attracted to each other."

Blue came closer. A smile threatened to break out on his face. "So it's your lustful soul you're concerned about."

"Stop it." The man could be a beast when he wanted.

"Really, Cassie, I would have thought you could exercise more control over your emotions." His face was only inches from hers. "Am I so tempting?"

Cassie's face turned a bright red. She knew he was purposely goading her. "You're about as tempting as day-old bread," she shot back.

"So what's the problem? As long as you can keep to your bedroom—"

"Oh, I despise your smugness," she said between gritted teeth.

He stepped even closer. "Yes, but there are a few things you like about me, or you wouldn't be running away."

There was that intoxicating male scent again, she noted. It made her head spin. "I don't have to run from the likes of you, Blue Mitchum." She saw the light in his eyes and knew he was laughing at her. Her temper simmering, she balled her fists at her sides. "I don't want Jenny Bowers's leftovers. Not to mention those of half the females in this town."

"You're beginning to sound jealous, Mrs. D'Clair," he said, reaching up to stroke her cheek. She flinched. "But let me assure you, none of those women could compete with you."

She raised her hand to slap him, and he caught her by the wrist. "How dare you compare me to the women who've climbed into the back of your car!"

Blue let her go with such a force, it almost sent her toppling. She grabbed the stair rail to steady herself. He looked disgusted. "Go ahead and run from me, Cassie. You're no different now than you were when you were growing up. But now I know you for what you really are, a snob. You're not worried about my career or your daughters' welfare. You're worried about yourself. Heaven forbid folks think you're sleeping with a half-breed."

"That's a lie!"

"I'm taking a shower. I don't care what you do," he said, his tone indifferent. "If you need a ride to the next town, I'll drive you. If you change your mind, then *you're* going to carry that luggage upstairs. I'm not going to run up and down the stairs with it like some bellhop. This isn't New York, princess. You don't reign supreme here." He turned and walked away, leaving Cassie speechless.

Feeling like a fool, she began carrying the luggage back upstairs. Tears stung her eyes, but she was determined not to cry. So Blue thought she was a snob. He thought the reason she stayed clear of him was that she was afraid someone might find out. He wasn't even close. The reason she avoided him was that she was terrified of getting close to another man. After her lousy marriage, she didn't want to become involved. But she would bite her tongue off before she confessed as much. If Blue found one vulnerable spot, he would use it to his advantage.

When Blue came out of his bedroom half an hour later, he noticed Cassie's bags were gone. He heard her moving around in the kitchen and smiled. It surprised him how much he liked the sound of her in his house.

The following morning Cassie spent much of her time interviewing two candidates for the housekeeping position. She took an instant liking to the second woman, who was named Mavis, and hired her on the spot. Mavis was tall and angular, but her warm smile kept her from looking severe.

"You understand this is a live-in position," Cassie said.

Mavis nodded. "That's fine by me. My husband died two years ago, and all my kids are grown."

Cassie introduced Mavis to the twins, and the woman went crazy over them. "Why, they're beautiful!"

"Thank you," Cassie said, and beamed proudly.

"Are they going to become famous models like their mama?"

Cassie rolled her eyes. "Not if I have anything to

say about it." She paused, then picked up the thread of their conversation. "When can you start? I'm only using Mr. Mitchum's upstairs until my parents return home. There's an extra bedroom next to mine you can use."

"I read in the newspaper that you plan to move into the old Kelsey home."

Cassie nodded. "Once the house is livable. I'm sure my parents can find room for us in the meantime. I'll need your help with the housekeeping as well as with tending to the girls from time to time."

"No problem. I have five children of my own and eight grandchildren. There's nothing I don't know about kids. As far as when I can start, I'll move in tomorrow, if that suits you. I've been living with my oldest son. I reckon he and his wife will be glad to have some privacy."

Cassie sighed her relief. For once it looked as though something was going to go off without a hitch. "That would be perfect. I'll see that your bedroom is ready."

Mavis frowned. "I'll take care of you, Mrs. D'Clair, you don't have to take care of me. I'll get my own bedroom ready."

Once Mavis was gone, Cassie checked her wristwatch and realized she was late for her appointment with the Suthers brothers. She ran outside to find Blue.

"Uh, I hate to bother you, Blue," she said hesitantly once she'd located him in the barn. "But would you mind driving me over to the house so I can meet with the Suthers brothers?" Cassie had avoided Blue since their argument the day before. "And later I really *do* need to buy a car," she said. "I'd appreciate your taking me to the next town to shop for one. Then I won't have to ask you to drive me places."

"Cassie, have I given you the impression that you bother me?" When she responded with a shake of her head, Blue went on, "Then stop apologizing, for heaven's sake. Why don't you get the keys off the dresser in my bedroom, gather up the girls, and I'll meet you at the jeep."

Cassie nodded and hurried toward the house. She crossed the den and hesitantly entered Blue's bedroom. She paused briefly inside the door. She had never been in Blue's bedroom before nor in the room he used as an office. She walked further into the room, taking in the mahogany four-poster bed and matching dresser and bureau. A simple multistriped bedspread of blue and rust covered the bed, but the walls were bare of pictures, as was most of the house. Cassie caught Blue's scent and her stomach fluttered wildly. She could imagine him naked and warm between the sheets, and that thought sent her heart racing. She found the keys and grabbed them with trembling hands, then left the room as though the devil himself were on her heels. She slammed right into Blue.

"Hey, where's the fire?"

Cassie blushed profusely. "I was just in a hurry, that's all." He was uncomfortably close. His scent enveloped her.

"I see you found the keys."

"Uh, yes." She held them up as evidence.

"Why are your hands trembling?" he asked.

"Huh? Oh, because I'm late for my appointment."

He gave her a knowing look. "I was afraid for a moment you might have been uncomfortable in my bedroom."

"I'm fine," she said, piqued that he could read her so easily.

"Good. Just don't forget where it is in case—" He paused. "You never know when you might need me in the middle of the night."

She would have had to be a dimwit not to catch his double meaning. "I doubt the occasion will arise," she said. "I'm a very capable woman."

"Is that the same as skillful?" he asked, one corner of his mouth turning up. It was obvious he was enjoying her discomfort.

Cassie bristled. "Let's get something straight, Blue—"

He waved her off. "I know, I know. You'd sooner sleep with vermin." He let himself out the front door, leaving Cassie behind.

Five

Bart and Dirk Suthers were sitting in their truck in front of Cassie's house when they arrived. Blue parked in the shade beneath a giant oak. The Suthers brothers opened their doors simultaneously and waited while Cassie made her way toward the house.

"Sorry I'm late," she said, walking briskly. Blue had offered to stay outside and watch the girls while she talked business. Cassie unlocked the door to the house. Despite the heat, the interior was cool. She headed for the kitchen with both men in tow. "You have the figures?" She turned around quickly and found both men staring at her slender legs. Cassie shot them a dark look.

Bart coughed as though embarrassed and laid several papers on the kitchen counter. "This is the best I could come up with, Mrs. . . . uh . . .

D'Clair. It's just a ballpark figure, of course. When you start tearing into a house this old, there's no tellin' what you'll find."

Cassie blinked at the figures before her. "But this is a lot of money!" she exclaimed. She wasn't about to tell them their figures were lower than the ones she'd received over the telephone from another contractor.

"Yes, ma'am," Bart agreed as Dirk nodded. "But that includes the roof, the wiring, the plumbing, not to mention the costs of sprucing up the place." At her blank look, he continued. "You know, stripping these here floors and having them varnished. Repairing the ceilings and roof. Painting the place. And the kitchen and bathrooms—"

"You don't have to remind me about the kitchen and bathrooms," she said grimly. She paced the floor in silence. "Can you hire several men to help you, so the job gets done faster?"

Bart hesitated. "It'll cost more."

"Hire as many men as you need, but I want this place completed as soon as possible. I'll pay time and a half for weekends."

She saw Bart and Dirk exchange looks. "That doesn't mean I want it slapped up so the slightest breeze knocks it down," she added. "I want the work done right." Both men shifted uneasily. Cassie wasn't used to asserting herself, but she'd be darned if she'd let a couple of contractors take advantage of her. She wasn't about to let *any* man take advantage of her, for that matter. "Also, you can count on seeing a lot of me. I want to make sure my money is spent well."

After a moment of silence, Bart spoke. "We'll start looking for independent contractors tomorrow. We can begin work the day after." He paused and pulled his trousers up over his belly. "Like I said, that quote is a ballpark figure. I allowed for nice fixtures and stuff, but if you start getting real fancy—"

"I understand."

He handed her another piece of paper. "I already made a list of what you'll need and the best places to buy things. Once the ceilings are repaired, you'll have to pick out your paint."

"Okay," Cassie said, "I want to check a few accomplished something since her return. "When do you need the money?"

"We ask for half at the signing of the contract and the other half once the job is done."

"Okay," Cassie said, "I want to check a few things, then we can plan to meet here the day after tomorrow. I'll sign the contracts and write you a check at that time." Bart nodded in agreement.

Cassie walked outside into the sunshine. Blue was sitting in the jeep, his gaze resting on the twins as they picked wildflowers in the tall grass surrounding the house. Once the girls spotted Cassie, both ran toward her, holding fistfuls of dandelions. She accepted them graciously, as though they were long-stemmed roses.

Blue started the engine once Cassie and the girls had seated themselves in the jeep. "Do you want to go by the grocery store?" he asked her.

Cassie looked up in surprise. She needed to go to the store, but she hadn't wanted to impose on

Blue any more than she already had. "If you don't mind. I need to buy groceries so I can work out a menu for Mavis."

"Mavis?" He arched both brows.

"Our new housekeeper. She's very nice. You'll like her."

Blue turned onto the main road and headed toward town. Cassie smiled as the breeze whipped through the interior of the jeep. In the back seat the girls giggled as the wind blew their hair around.

Cassie couldn't contain her excitement over having her house restored. She planned to phone the Builders' Association and check out the Suthers brothers before she signed the contract, but Bart had given her several references. As it stood, it looked as though she had found herself a couple of reliable contractors.

When they reached the main part of town, Cassie spotted the bank and remembered she had business there. "Could you drop me by the bank?" she asked Blue. "I need to open a checking account. I've already called and they have everything ready for me to sign." Blue nodded and turned into the parking lot. "I'll be right back," Cassie said, climbing out of the jeep. She hurried in.

Once inside, Cassie was ushered to the manager's office, where everything had been readied for her as promised. She didn't miss the stares and whispers the tellers and customers gave her, however.

"Welcome home, Cassie," Ed Calhoun, the bank manager, said. Cassie had grown up with his daughter and felt comfortable with Ed. She went into his arms easily, and he hugged her. "It's nice to have a celebrity living among us," he continued.

Cassie smiled. "I'm not a celebrity anymore, Mr. Calhoun—"

"Call me Ed."

"I'm just an ordinary mother now." Cassie asked about her friend as she selected checks. She signed her name and was given a book of counter checks while she listened to Ed as he updated her on the news of his family.

"Come by when you can stay longer," Ed said, once Cassie turned down the offer of a cup of coffee. She waved and hurried out the front door.

"That was fast," Blue said, starting the ignition. He pulled onto the road.

Blue parked his jeep in the Piggly Wiggly parking lot a few minutes later. He climbed out, then helped the girls. Cassie stepped out on the other side, found a shopping cart, and started rolling it toward the store, making sure the girls were beside her. Blue found a cart as well and pushed it up behind Cassie. She came to a halt. "What are you doing? We agreed that I would buy the groceries."

Blue eyed her steadily. "I never verbally agreed to anything, and I'm not letting you foot the bill. We can split it."

Cassie knew arguing with him would be a waste of time. But she also knew the last thing she needed was for another man to take charge of her and the girls—especially Blue Mitchum. She didn't want to be indebted to a man like him. Cassie pushed her cart inside the store. She wasn't being fair, she told herself. Blue had been a good host. The fact that she'd had disastrous luck with men was no reason to blame him. Still . . . She would have to watch herself around Blue. No man could be as good-looking as he was without being a little untrustworthy.

Cassie went about buying groceries while at the same time watching Blue out of the corner of her eye. The girls had him parked on the candy aisle, and from the looks of it, Blue was being suckered into buying most of what they pointed to. "You don't have to buy all that," Cassie said, pulling up next to him. "Besides, I don't let them eat much candy." Both girls moaned.

Blue gave them a stern look. "You heard your mother. You can each choose a bag you like, and it'll be up to your mom to decide when you can have it." Each girl picked her favorite, and Blue tossed the packages into the cart. Cassie shot him a grateful look.

As she shopped, Cassie would have had to be blind not to notice the glances Blue received from many of the women in the store. She couldn't help but wonder how many of the women he knew personally. A tiny spark of jealousy came to life inside her, but she squelched it. She had no claim on Blue, she told herself. If she wanted to start a new life in Peculiar, she'd have to get that fact through her head.

At the cash register, Blue and Cassie each wrote a check for half the amount. The cashier, who couldn't have been more than sixteen, never took her eyes off Blue. Cassie's reaction to the smile Blue gave the girl startled her.

"Must you do that?" Cassie asked Blue as they rolled their carts toward the jeep.

Blue looked up in surprise. "Do what?"

"Gawk at every female who crosses your path. That poor girl is still in high school, for heaven's sake."

"I was merely returning a smile."

"You were leering."

Blue threw his head back and laughed. "Why, Mrs. D'Clair, I think you're jealous," he taunted.

"That'll be the day," she said, trying to convince herself as well as him.

Blue parked his cart beside the jeep and began unloading bags. Then he helped the girls in. "You can put your feet on the seat," he told them. "There's no room on the floor." Somehow he managed to fit the girls in among the grocery bags.

Cassie insisted on helping Blue unload their purchases when they got home. "I picked up several steaks," he said. "I thought I would cook them on the grill."

Cassie was pleased by his thoughtfulness. "I'll prepare the baked potatoes and salad." She began scrubbing baking potatoes while Blue marinated the steaks. Every time Blue reached around her to get something out of the drawer, his arm brushed hers. Cassie held her breath each time. After a while, she realized he was doing it on purpose, and she moved to another spot, unaware of the grin Blue had on his face.

"I'd better check on the girls again," Cassie said, once she'd finished washing the potatoes. "I wonder where they are this time?"

"Where do you think?"

"Playing with the kittens?"

Blue nodded.

"I suppose I'll have to let them have one when we move into the house," she said. "They've never had a pet before."

"You're kidding."

She shook her head. "Their father was allergic to animal fur." She shrugged. "Besides, we were on the go constantly, so it wouldn't have made sense to have a pet."

"Frankly, I would have gotten rid of the husband and bought a pet."

Although Cassie secretly agreed, she shot him an it's-none-of-your-business look. She of all people knew she'd made a mistake by marrying Jean-François. She had come to the conclusion that her attraction to him had been based on sheer loneliness—but then, she'd been just as lonely after the marriage.

"Penny for your thoughts," Blue said. Cassie looked so forlorn that he thought she might cry.

"I was just thinking how badly I've screwed up my life," she said, surprised she could be so honest with him. She hadn't had anyone she could talk to in years. Her busy schedule had kept her from making close friends. Something told her, though, that she could confide in Blue. "I've put my daughters through hell," Cassie choked out. "They'll never have a relationship with their father."

Blue went to her and grasped her gently by the shoulders. "It's all right," he said. "The girls don't look as though they've suffered. Both are normal and healthy."

"Tara's too quiet."

"She's shy."

"I worry about her."

"You're her mother, that's your job." He smiled down at her. Cassie's eyes teared. "Please don't cry," he said. "I can't handle a weeping woman."

Cassie swallowed the lump in her throat. "I'm sorry." She felt his hands burn through the fabric of her blouse. They were big and comforting. She looked into his eyes and was taken aback once again by their light blue color. His face was dark and handsome, each feature etched to perfection. No wonder he drove the women wild, she thought. His lips caught and held her attention. She already knew how wonderful they tasted, how marvelous they felt against her own. Before she realized what was happening, his lips descended onto hers.

Cassie stopped breathing as Blue's mouth made contact with her own. His scent permeated her senses, making her giddy and heightening her own ardor. Cassie opened her mouth for him. His tongue seemed to have a mind of its own. It was hot and demanding, prodding her mouth open wider in its quest. Cassie felt a heat spread through her body. It settled low in her belly, giving her pleasure while at the same time making her restless.

When Blue raised his mouth from hers, they

both sighed. He rained light kisses across her face. "Damn, you taste good," he said, his throaty voice sending shivers through her. "I'd like to taste you all over."

Cassie thought her legs were going to buckle beneath her. Just the thought of Blue Mitchum making love to her with his lips was enough to make her head spin. She knew without being told that he would be a considerate lover. "Blue, I don't think—"

"You want me to make love to you, too, don't you, Cassie? I can read it in your face. Why do you deny it?"

Cassie saw desire in his eyes. She pulled back slightly. "I'm not about to become involved with anyone after what I've been through."

Blue smiled. "Who says you have to get involved?"

Cassie stiffened. His insinuation was clear. "Forgive me. I forgot who I was dealing with for a moment."

"I can make you forget your troubles, Cassie. I've wanted you since you were fifteen, but you were too young. You're a woman now."

Cassie shook free from him. "Forget it, Blue. I don't do one-night stands."

"Who said anything about one-night stands?" He paused. "What do you want, Cassie? Someone who will make false promises to you? Didn't you learn anything from your messed-up marriage? I'll give it to you straight. We'll both know where we stand."

"I have to check the girls," she said, starting for the door.

"You're running away from me again, Cassie," he said, following her. "What are you afraid of?"

She didn't answer him. He watched the gentle sway of her hips as she made her way toward the barn. Desire stirred through his loins as he fantasized for a moment. Her skin would be soft as a baby's, her perfume an aphrodisiac to his senses. He'd gone upstairs that morning to help Bree find her sneakers and had marveled at the bottles of creams and lotions sitting on the bureau. He'd found her perfume and sniffed it, knowing it was expensive just by the smell.

"Mommy puts that stuff on before she goes to bed," Bree had informed him, pulling one sneaker from under a neat pile of dirty clothes that Cassie had planned to sort later. "I think it's silly, don't you?"

"Oh, yes," Blue had agreed quickly. "I would never smear all that junk on me. I'm surprised your mother doesn't slide right out of bed." They had both laughed as they searched for the remaining sneaker, but Blue couldn't concentrate. What he wouldn't give to rub those lotions on her naked body himself. Now, as he watched her, he could only imagine how wonderful it would be.

Cassie found the twins in the barn playing with the kittens, just as Blue had said. "Mind if I join you?" she asked. Both girls looked up.

"Mommy, look at this kitty," Tara said, holding up a black-and-white kitten. "Can I have it?"

Cassie smiled and knelt beside them. "You may have it once we move into our house. Of course, you'll have to ask Mr. Mitchum."

Tara was obviously pleased. Bree held up a calico for inspection. "This is the one I want, Mommy."

Cassie nodded and reached over to stroke the mother cat, who purred in response. She was thankful she had escaped Blue's arms. With her daughters she felt safe. Blue stirred up too many emotions, emotions that were new and exciting to her, while at the same time terrifying. Once again she reminded herself: she had to keep her distance.

Blue eyed Cassie all through dinner. She was polite but aloof. When it came time for the girls to go to bed, Cassie excused herself as well. She didn't miss the look of disappointment on Blue's face. That same face swam before her when she closed her eyes to sleep.

Mavis arrived just as Cassie and Blue were having their first cup of coffee. Cassie introduced her to Blue.

The woman shook Blue's hand, then got down to business. "Now, where are the two little angels I met yesterday?" she asked.

"They're sleeping in this morning. We're enjoying the silence."

"What do they like for breakfast?"

"Pancakes, when I'm in the mood to make them," Cassie said. "Otherwise, they eat cereal and toast."

"Then I will make them a tall stack of buttermilk pancakes." Mavis reached into her purse and pulled out a bib apron.

"You don't need to spoil them," Cassie said.

"Trust me. I know all about children. My children turned out good. Never had any trouble with them at school." She paused. "Your little girls will turn out good too. Just wait and see."

"I'm sorry I didn't make a list of what needs to be done around here," Cassie said, changing the subject. "I ran out of time and—"

"No worry. I know what to do. I been cleaning folks' houses for years." She opened a cabinet and pulled out a mixing bowl.

"Is she for real?" Blue whispered.

Cassie nodded. "That's why I hired her on the spot."

The Suthers brothers had hired three men, and the place was alive with activity. Two days after Cassie signed the contract, a truck bearing lumber and roof shingles arrived. Neither Bart nor Dirk Suthers had time to answer her questions as they unloaded the vehicle and supervised the men. Cassie realized they had ordered and received material in record time. She was certain it had something to do with the bonus she had offered—that and the fact that the Suthers brothers were related to the man who owned the lumberyard.

Cassie decided to drive herself to town and look at some of the items she would need for the house. After several days of lessons, Blue thought she was capable of driving alone. She set out to buy light fixtures and ceiling fans, and returned a couple of hours later, pleased with herself and for having stayed within her budget. As she pulled the jeep into the driveway, Blue came out to meet her. "How would you and the girls like to ride to the next town to look for a car?" he suggested.

Cassie was more than agreeable, since she didn't want to keep putting Blue out by borrowing his jeep—although he never seemed to mind. "Can you give me forty-five minutes to clean up and dress?"

He nodded and checked his wristwatch. "We could have a late lunch."

Mavis offered to watch the girls, neither of whom had any desire to drive around looking for cars. Once Cassie had lectured them thoroughly about being on their best behavior, Blue urged her out the front door. "We're only going to the next town for a few hours," he reminded her.

"Yes, but they tend to get into trouble if they're not watched constantly."

Blue rolled his eyes. "Tell me about it. This morning they tied all their ribbons on Pippin's mane and tail. It's a good thing he's gentle, but now he looks as though he's going to be in a parade. I drew the line when Bree wanted to paint his hooves with your fingernail polish."

"Oh, no."

"Oh, yes."

"I don't know how you manage to hold on to your patience."

He laughed. "I have my moments. But just when I feel like wringing their little necks, they give me this innocent we-didn't-do-it look, and I turn to jelly."

Cassie laughed sympathetically. "I know it's been tough on you. I hope Mavis can keep them out of mischief." They looked at each other doubtfully. Blue drove some distance before pulling up in front of a small restaurant. "You like barbecued food?"

"I love it. But it's so fattening," she added guiltily.

"Give me a break," Blue said. "I'll see if they have some melba toast you can munch on while I eat a real meal."

"Forget it, mister. I can eat my weight in ribs." She let him help her out of the car and open the door to the restaurant. Although the place wasn't very impressive to look at, the aromas emanating from the kitchen made Cassie's mouth water. Blue escorted her to one of the big wooden booths in the back, and a waitress wearing jeans and a baggy T-shirt handed them menus.

"So what's going on at the house?" Blue asked after they'd ordered and were waiting to be served.

"I went into town and picked out some of the fixtures on the list," she said. "I was surprised to find a lot of what I needed in Peculiar, but I still have several more items to pick out."

Cassie felt a bit self-conscious. Blue hadn't taken his eyes off her lips since she'd begun talking. She fidgeted with her hands under the table. Blue was wearing new jeans, and his white short-sleeved knit shirt emphasized his dark coloring and powerful chest. Cassie had chosen a simple yellow tank top with a matching wraparound skirt. A deep V in the tank top was inset with yellow and white stripes, and she wore a pair of big white earrings.

"You look nice," Blue said, his gaze dropping to the V of her tank top. "But then, you always do."

"Thank you. You look pretty good yourself."

"Just good?" He had a teasing gleam in his eyes.

She pursed her lips. "Don't get smug."

"You look good enough to eat," he responded. "And you smell like a slice of heaven. Why don't we say to hell with shopping for a car and—"

"Don't say it," she interrupted. "Don't even think it." She paused. "The answer is no."

Blue's eyes were bright with humor. "How can you say no when I haven't even told you my idea?"

Cassie was about to answer him, when the waitress arrived with their food. Blue didn't seem particularly interested in his meal; his gaze lingered on Cassie's face.

She picked up a rib and chewed, taking in her surroundings with great interest—anything to keep from meeting those stark blue eyes across the table.

"You're just putting off the inevitable," Blue said, starting on his own lunch. "You know we're going to . . . uh . . . get together. The question is, when?"

Cassie almost choked. She gave him a suspicious look. "Do you have any intention of taking me to shop for a car, or is this one of your famous seduction techniques? I have to admit, it's different."

He ignored the question. "How did you end up with violet-blue eyes? Nobody in your family has them."

"You're changing the subject."

"Sometimes at night, when the light hits them just right, they look almost purple. Did you know that?"

"Yes. After hundreds of modeling jobs, I'm aware of that fact."

"Wonder what color they turn when you're making love."

Cassie's food went down the wrong way, and she fell into a fit of coughing. Her face turned a bright red. Blue stood quickly and patted her on the back until she was able to swallow. She blushed at some of the looks she received from other customers.

"Are you okay?" Blue asked, concern etched on his face.

Tears ran down her cheeks. "You deliberately try to shock or embarrass me constantly," she said harshly.

He grinned. "You're right. But I don't want you to get all choked up over it."

"Then answer one thing. If you're so damn certain I'm going to come crawling into your bedroom, why do you insist on badgering me with sexual innuendo?"

"Have you ever tried to get a tractor started?"

Cassie's face went completely blank at the sudden change in subject. "What does that have to do with me?"

"You can never get the engine started on the first attempt," he said. "You have to prime it, play with it a bit before it comes to life. Women are like that."

"You're comparing me to a tractor?" she said in disbelief, then didn't give him time to answer. "You certainly know how to charm a girl. Why, I'm just weak-kneed over your flattery."

"Why should I waste my time on silly chatter that doesn't mean anything?" he asked. "Women have sexual urges just as men—"

"Not here, Blue."

"Are you denying it? Was your sex life fulfilling with the Frenchman—"

"I said stop it!" Cassie said between gritted teeth. "My love life is none of your business. Sometimes a woman just wants to be held, Blue. It doesn't matter who's holding her as long as it locks out the loneliness for a while. Has that ever occurred to you? No, I can see that it hasn't. This conversation is finished." She tossed her napkin onto her plate on top of her half-eaten lunch.

"Where are you going?" he asked, surprised.

"I'll wait for you in the car." She was up from her seat and out the door before he could stop her.

Blue tossed his own napkin down and sighed in self-disgust. Why did he insist on damaging whatever kind of relationship Cassie and he had? She was a lady. First-class. He wasn't used to that. Most of the women he knew were just out for a good time. Yes, but he could learn how to treat a lady, he told himself. He'd had to learn how to make decisions and speeches and change his ways in his role as mayor. Surely he could learn to act like a gentleman with a woman if he had to, he decided.

The ride to the next town was made in silence. Cassie stared out her window at the passing scenery while Blue concentrated on driving. Every now and then he shot her a quick glance. Once they arrived in Fairfield, Blue drove to the section of town lined with car dealerships. When Blue stopped at a red light, Cassie noticed a sign for a Mercedes dealer.

Blue frowned. "That's the last thing you need, living out in the country," he said. "You need something that you can use to haul stuff in."

Blue's words struck a chord within her. He sounded exactly like Jean-François. "Turn in, please," Cassie said, once the light had changed.

"Are you serious?"

"I make my own decisions, Blue," she said matter-of-factly.

Blue shook his head as though the woman had lost all common sense. "It's your money," he said tightly.

She smiled. "Yes, it is, isn't it?"

Two hours later, after closing the deal, Cassie left the lot the proud owner of a cream-colored Mercedes station wagon. While she had followed a salesman from car to car, Blue had sat in the lobby reading magazines, a frown creasing his brow. Now, as he drove Cassie home, she was pleased with her decision to buy the car. Although she had intended to purchase a four-wheel-drive vehicle, she would have bought a horse and buggy before letting Blue Mitchum tell her what to do. He had a lot to learn about women, she decided. And it pleased her to know she had just given him his first lesson. She couldn't wait until all the paperwork was processed and she could pick up the car.

Six

Cassie muttered curses as the sheet of wallpaper fell loose from the bathroom ceiling onto her head. Sweat trickled down the back of her neck and between her breasts from the effort. "Damn wallpaper," she said aloud. "Damn bathroom," she added between clenched teeth. "Why couldn't they have built a normal bathroom instead of a rotunda?" She peered out from beneath the wallpaper in frustration. Trying to make the paper adhere to the curved surface was proving hopeless. She stifled the urge to tear the long sheet of paper to shreds.

"Knock, knock," a male voice called out from the other side of the bathroom door, which was ajar to keep the room from getting hot. Blue pushed the door open wider and arched both brows when he saw Cassie. "What are you doing?"

"I'm vacationing in the Bahamas," she said tightly. "What does it look like I'm doing?"

"You don't know much about putting up wallpaper, do you?"

Her patience at an end, she bit out her words. "I don't have a Ph.D. in it, if that's what you mean."

Blue came into the room. "Here, let me hold it for a minute. Your arms must be getting tired."

Cassie was relieved to let go, and she climbed down the stepladder. "Thanks, Blue. It's this blasted wall," she said. "How am I supposed to wallpaper something that looks as if it were designed by a medieval architect?"

"Very carefully," he said. "Where's your paste?"

"On the kitchen counter. I've been using it as my work space. You wouldn't believe how long each sheet of paper has to be cut."

"Bring me the paste and a brush."

"Why?"

"Just do it."

Cassie didn't argue. She was back in a matter of seconds, holding a pail of paste and a large paintbrush. Blue, still holding the paper, dabbed the brush into the pail and swiped it on sections of the paper that were beginning to dry. "It would have been a lot simpler to paint this room," he said. Blue pressed the paper against the wall first, then carried it across the ceiling to the other side, where he met a flat wall. "Hand me that sponge."

Cassie studied each step with a critical eye. "You have paper hanging from the curve."

"Just give me the sponge," he said curtly.

"Yes, sir!"

Blue smoothed the paper on the wall, then carefully ran it over the curve. The extra paper adhered to it, and he rubbed the air pockets away gently. Cassie was dumbfounded. "You weren't allowing enough paper for the curve," he said. He stepped back and looked at it.

"Where did you learn to wallpaper?" Cassie asked, still awed by the way he made it look so easy.

"There's not much I don't know how to do, Mrs. D'Clair," he said. "To keep food in my belly I've done everything from washing dishes to shoveling cow dung." He paused, a cocky tilt to his head. "Of course, I do my best work in the dark."

"I'm surprised," she said.

"Oh?"

"I would expect someone like you to have mirrors and spotlights, so you could gloat over your own expertise."

"Hmm. I've never used mirrors. Perhaps you could advise me on where I should have them installed. I can just imagine your reflection—"

"Don't." It was a simple but direct remark. "Don't place me in your fantasies, because you're only going to end up disappointed."

"Why, are you that bad in the sack?"

"Please leave. As you see, I have work to do."

"Why are *you* doing this when there are qualified people to do it for you?"

"Because I felt like being useful. Mavis has taken

over the housework, and the girls are off playing. I *have* to do something."

He nodded as though he understood. "I like your choice of colors. What do you call them?"

"Mint green and salmon. It'll match the rest of my furnishings when they arrive." She left the room and went back into the kitchen, where she measured another long sheet of paper.

"You need to cut it an inch or so longer so you can match the pattern," Blue said.

"I know that," she lied.

"Want some help? I can have your bathroom wallpapered in no time flat."

She looked suspicious. "Why would you want to help me wallpaper my bathroom?" He tilted his dark head to one side in a manner that was beginning to do strange things to her insides.

" 'Cause I'm a nice guy."

"Not good enough."

He sighed. "Okay, I need a favor."

She crossed her arms. "Why am I not surprised? Forget it, I don't exchange sexual favors. I don't care if it takes me the rest of my life to wallpaper this room."

"Why, Mrs. D'Clair, I am truly shocked!" Blue said, his eyes twinkling. "I hope you're not suggesting I would crawl low enough to help a lady in distress in exchange for sex."

"No, I'm not suggesting it, I'm stating a fact." She glanced up from her work and saw that he looked serious. "Okay, what's the favor?" Darn, the man could get her to agree to just about anything when he looked at her like that.

"I need a date. I'm involved in a fund-raising project, and the dinner is tonight."

"Oh? Are you trying to have a bordello built next to city hall?" she asked with a smile.

"This is for real, Cassie. It's a dinner held to raise money for elderly shut-ins. We hope to get something started like Meals on Wheels as well as volunteer medical assistants to check them regularly. Also, I'll be asking folks to sign up to visit one shut-in on a daily basis."

Cassie felt about an inch tall after hearing Blue's explanation. It dawned on her suddenly that there were sides to the man she hadn't seen. She was accustomed to his carefree sexual banter, not this serious side that was devoted to helping the community.

"And you can't find a date?" she asked as though he'd just told her the world wasn't round, as everybody thought, but flat as a pancake. "I don't believe it."

"I never said I couldn't find a date, princess. Let's just say I'm getting a bit picky about whom I go out with."

"Think we can finish wallpapering the bathroom in time?" she asked, not wanting him to see the excitement in her eyes. She was still embarrassed over the snide remarks she'd made. She just wasn't used to the new Blue Mitchum.

"The dinner doesn't start till eight o'clock, but I think I would wallpaper faster if you weren't wearing those shorts and that tank top."

"It's hot in here," she protested.

"Damn right it is," he said, noting that her nipples were visible beneath her top.

Three hours later, the bathroom was papered. Blue stood atop the stepladder in front of the closed door, making sure he had trimmed each spot in a straight line. Cassie couldn't help but notice his lean thighs and slim hips as he worked. She would be relieved to escape the close confines of the bathroom. The sexual tension had been thick enough to slice as she and Blue worked together.

Blue climbed down the ladder and looked around. "What do you think?"

"You did a wonderful job," she said. "Do you really like the colors I chose?" For some reason his opinion was important to her.

He nodded. "I don't know much about decorating, but I think the colors look good together. You seem to have a flair for matching things. You're not thinking about going into interior decorating, are you?"

She laughed. "No. I only know what *I* like. I haven't the slightest idea what other people prefer."

"I think I like just about everything about you." There was a teasing lilt to his voice, but he felt as though his blood pressure had risen considerably in the past few hours. With Cassie standing on the stepladder holding the wallpaper while he tried to concentrate on gluing it to the walls, he'd literally dripped sweat. Her thighs and legs, not to mention her pert fanny, which had been at his eye level most of the time, had tempted him beyond rational thought. More than once he had stifled the urge to let go of the wallpaper and bury his face against her. He was thankful when she'd climbed down.

Cassie had no idea what Blue was thinking because her mind was filled with her own thoughts. She finally decided to voice them. "Blue, I'm sorry for the nasty comments I made earlier," she said. "I don't know why we have to knock heads constantly."

He stepped closer and looked into her eyes. "I do, Cassie. It's because we're so damned attracted to each other. You can deny it if you like, but I know what I see in your eyes." Without warning, he slipped his arms around her waist and pulled her closer.

Though surprised, Cassie was mesmerized by the look on his face. "I should never have moved into your house," she said more to herself than to him. "This wouldn't have happened if I had been able to find another place to stay."

"What's wrong with what's happening between us, Cassie?" he asked gently. "Is it my past?" He almost whispered the next sentence. "Is it my heritage?"

"Don't be ridiculous. If I fell in love with a man, I wouldn't care if he was half moose. I told you before, it's me."

"You've had time to get over your divorce," he said. "Surely you aren't pining away over that Frenchman."

"I just don't want to be used or hurt again, Blue."

"And you think I'd do that to you?"

"I don't know. I would never be able to give myself to a man if he couldn't be faithful to me in return." She dropped her gaze.

Blue lifted her chin until she was looking directly into his eyes. "I'll admit I was wild in my younger days and that I still find women attractive, but I haven't committed any great sin."

"What do you mean?"

"I'm a free agent, Cassie. I have never made a commitment to a woman. Until I do, I see nothing wrong with my life-style."

All at once the room seemed to fill with Blue's presence—his touch, his smell, his mere existence. Cassie was overwhelmed. "I . . . I don't think you're the type of man who could make a commitment," she said.

He pondered the thought. "I'll admit the woman would have to be pretty special."

Cassie tried to step back, but Blue tightened his grip on her. "Kiss me, Cassie."

Her heart leapt to her throat. "Blue . . ."

"I've chased you since you returned. I've stolen kisses whenever possible. Now I want you to kiss me and tell me if you like it."

"I don't think that's a good idea."

His look challenged her. "Unless you're afraid you can't handle it."

"Of course I can handle it," she said adamantly. "I'm not fifteen years old anymore, and you don't intimidate me."

"Then what are you waiting for?"

Cassie took a deep breath and placed her hands

on his shoulders. This is insane, she thought. Still, the idea was tempting. She stood on tiptoe and touched his lips with hers. Although she had planned to kiss him lightly and be done with it, Blue snaked his arms around her waist and anchored her against his body. The kiss deepened. Blue opened his mouth, a silent invitation for her to explore it with her tongue. She did so shyly, but he used his own tongue boldly. Her head was spinning from the taste of him.

Blue broke the kiss and pressed his lips against the hollow of her throat. He smiled at the erratic pounding he felt there, and knew the kiss had thrilled her as much as it had him. "There are so many ways I want to make love to you, Cassie," he whispered, his lips inching their way to her earlobe. "There are so many things I want to learn about your body." His breath was hot on her cheek. "What color are your nipples?"

Cassie wasn't prepared for the question, but the look in his eyes compelled her to answer. It was like being in a trance. "I don't know," she said, her own voice sounding far away. "I guess they're a dark pink. Coral maybe?" She blanched. What had made her answer something so personal? Had another man asked, she would have slapped him soundly on the face. What power did Blue wield over her that made her so vulnerable to him?

"I want to see your breasts, Cassie. I've wanted to see them for years. I want to stroke each one until your nipples become hard."

"Blue, don't say any more." Cassie shivered. It was all too much for her.

The sound of her voice startled him. He leaned back and gazed into eyes that had deepened in color, eyes that glistened with unshed tears. "What is it, Cassie? Am I going too fast for you?" When she nodded, he cursed himself. "I'm sorry, baby. It's just . . . well, you're so damn beautiful. I can't help but want to make love to you."

"I know. I want you to make love to me, too, Blue," she confessed. "But there are too many 'what ifs.' I don't want to be hurt again. I don't want my girls to witness the suffering I went through with their father."

"Cassie, I would never hurt you," he said solemnly.

"Yes, you would," she said, giving him a sad smile. "You may have changed in a lot of ways, but you're still attracted to a pretty face. Not only that, you would start making all my decisions for me. I would be right back where I started."

"Oh, Cassie, no."

"I need time. I came here to build a new life with my daughters, and that's exactly what I plan to do. The last thing I need to do is involve myself in a relationship that wouldn't stand a chance."

He sighed heavily, closed his eyes, and leaned his head back, wondering how long he could remain sane from wanting her. He was a man who always got what he wanted when he wanted it. But not with Cassie. Sweet, lovable, sexy Cassie. There was no convincing her. She had always been out of his grasp. When he spoke, his voice sounded stilted, resigned. "I'll back off if you want me to. Perhaps that would be less frustrating." He released her and let himself out of the room without looking back.

The high-school cafeteria had been chosen for the fund-raising dinner meeting. At least a dozen women had been working all day in the kitchen, frying chicken and making homemade biscuits. Blue and Cassie arrived early to make sure all was in order. They found several citizens hard at work, putting cloths and flowers on the tables.

"I may need your help once people start coming in," Blue whispered. "You can either take the money or make name tags."

"I've always been good with money," she said, a teasing lilt in her voice.

Blue's smile was stiff. They had been uncomfortable with each other since the incident in the bathroom, but he couldn't help but appreciate the picture she made. She looked adorable in a cotton plaid skirt of peach, khaki, and tan. A lightweight knit blouse in the same peach hue brought color to her cheeks. Big square earrings were her only jewelry. Although Blue had chosen to dress in a blue business suit, he suspected Cassie had purposely tried to dress as casually as she could in order to fit in with the townsfolk. He was certain her closet was filled with designer silks, but it looked as though she was determined not to stand out in the crowd. He almost laughed at the thought. She would stand out dressed in burlap.

Cassie seemed to be pondering something. "Why the serious look?" Blue asked.

"I think perhaps I'll collect the money," she whispered. "As much as I hate to admit it, I've forgotten a lot of names."

He nodded his understanding. "You'll pick them up. Just give yourself time." He handed her a metal box. "There's change already in there. The dinner is eight-fifty a head. Half the proceeds go to the project."

Cassie nodded and took a seat next to an old high-school acquaintance. They conversed easily as the crowd started filing in through the door. It was obvious the women were a bit taken with Cassie's presence. Blue stood beside the table and shook hands, welcoming each person who came in through the door. Cassie wondered how he could remember so many names, but then, Blue had lived in Peculiar all his life, she realized. She was overwhelmed as folks started welcoming her home. After her fast-paced life in New York, the simplicity and warmth of the hometown crowd touched her.

Once the room was filled to capacity, Blue led Cassie to the head table and seated her. He welcomed several of his staff, then took the seat beside her. Dinner was served, and everyone chatted amicably while they ate. Cassie recognized many faces, although some made her draw a blank. She was very much aware of Blue's presence beside her, but a woman would have to be deaf, dumb, and blind not to, she thought. Seeing Blue Mitchum in a suit did a number on her nervous system.

"I wonder if the girls have bound and gagged Mavis yet?" she whispered, thankful the twins had taken a liking to the woman.

Blue looked amused. "Something tells me that Mavis can handle just about anything. Even your girls," he added with a smile that almost knocked the breath out of her.

Once dinner wound down and a dessert of strawberry shortcake was served, Blue excused himself and crossed the platform to speak with the other men. at the rear of the room, a large film projector was wheeled in. Blue pulled down a giant white screen from a metal frame that hung behind the podium. While the townsfolk looked on curiously, Blue made his way over to the podium, turned on the microphone, and tapped it several times. It squealed once.

"Can everybody hear me?" he asked. There were nods throughout the room. "Okay." He looked satisfied. "First, I'd like to thank each and every one of you for coming tonight. I'd also like to thank those responsible for helping with the event." He pointed to a group of ladies lined up beside the kitchen door wearing bib aprons. "I think we should give these lovely ladies a big hand for spending the day in a hot kitchen preparing such a delicious meal." The crowd applauded, as did Blue, and the ladies beamed.

Once the noise died down, Blue became serious. "When I became mayor of this town, I promised that we would work together as a family to see that everyone in our town would have his needs met." He leaned on the podium. "I confess I made that statement out of naiveté. I had no idea a town this size would have so many needs." He paused. "Each time I've come to you for help, you've given generously. In three years, we've tackled some tough issues . . ."

Cassie listened attentively to what Blue was saying. She would never have guessed him to be such a good speaker, yet he had the rapt attention of everyone in the room. Not only that, there was an air of respect and trust directed at him that surprised her most of all. Had she concentrated so hard on Blue's bad-boy past that she couldn't see the goodness of the man he'd become?

". . . Together we organized a home for troubled teens under the direction of counselors and volunteers. We now have various private shelters located throughout the town to house battered women." Blue paused as the crowd applauded. He continued. "We have a twenty-four-hour crisis hotline, operated solely by volunteers." More applause. "And we became more responsible for the welfare of homeless animals and worked with the shelters to see that necessary funds were raised to feed these animals." He paused and looked across the sea of faces. "Because we raised public awareness, the animal shelter has reported a much lower incidence of unwanted cats and dogs." He paused once more while the crowd applauded again.

"Before I get to tonight's topic, I'd like to re-mind you of what I told you from the beginning. When you applaud me, you are actually applauding your own efforts. If it were not for the generosity of the people of this town, we would never have come this far. I thank you for that."

Cassie accepted a cup of coffee from one of the volunteer workers, but her eyes were focused on Blue. She had been more or less isolated since her return and knew nothing of Blue's success. It was obvious he cared a great deal about Peculiar.

"The reason I called you here tonight is to talk about another problem that has come to my at-tention." It was obvious he had the crowd right where he wanted them.

"Several members of my staff have discovered there are a number of elderly shut-ins who for one reason or another have nobody to care for them. Presently we know of at least twenty-five persons in our town. These people don't get hot meals, and most of them can't afford many groceries on their social-security checks. They go for days with-out seeing another face unless they happen to spot the mailman. They are prisoners in their own homes. They can't attend church or other social events." Blue stopped short. "I think in-stead of my trying to explain their plight, the film you are about to see will do a much better job. Afterward, we will open up the meeting for dis-cussion." He moved the podium aside so the screen was visible. The crowd had suddenly gone silent. The lights were turned off as people waited expec-tantly.

Once he joined her, Cassie stared at Blue as if seeing him for the first time. In the darkened room he did not notice her look of glowing pride. "You need to turn your chair around so you can see the screen," he whispered.

"You were wonderful," she whispered in return.

"Thanks." He was surprised by the compliment, especially since he knew Cassie had probably listened to many professional speakers. He had never considered himself a great orator; he more or less winged it. Sometimes he took notes for his speeches if he had to go over budgets, but most of the time he just spoke what he felt. He knew the townspeople well enough to know they would frown on flowery words. They came to the meetings to find out what was happening in their town. They preferred the simple truth. Blue always tried to deliver.

"You really take your job seriously," Cassie said, interrupting his thoughts.

"I wouldn't be here if I didn't."

The projector started and for the next twenty minutes everyone in the room watched as the film illustrated the suffering of the elderly. Cassie felt a lump in her throat the size of an egg, and her eyes misted. Life had been good for her, despite her unhappiness with Jean-François. She had always had plenty to eat and a warm place to sleep, as had her children. Her heart ached for those who had to do without.

When the film was over, the lights were turned on, but Blue remained in his seat. He wanted people to absorb what they'd seen. Many would be shocked, but his gut told him the people of Peculiar would not allow such atrocities in their town. After several minutes, he stood and moved the podium back into place, switching on the microphone once more.

"I didn't ask you here tonight to depress you," Blue said solemnly. "I watched the film myself several times and debated whether or not to show it because of the subject matter." He looked around the room at a sea of grim faces.

"In the three years since I took office, I have tried to be honest and sincere. As the saying goes, sometimes the truth hurts. As a family, I ask that you help end the hunger and isolation some of our elderly experience daily. As in the past, I challenge you once again to rally yourselves for another cause." He paused. "Because one of those persons could be your own mother or father."

Blue stacked several sheets of paper together as the crowd applauded. A number of people in the audience got up, giving him a standing ovation. Once the noise died down, he faced them once again. "Are there any questions?" he asked. All meetings were carried out on a casual basis. Blue frowned on parliamentary procedure, simply because folks seemed hesitant to speak under formal conditions.

Edgar Aldridge, who owned the local hardware store, stood. Blue acknowledged him with a nod. "I'd like to know just how soon we can organize a committee to take care of this problem," Edgar said. "My wife has just volunteered to take on one shut-in, and I'm going to donate five hundred dollars from my hardware store." A hush filled the room. Edgar glanced around. "I challenge the rest of you to follow your consciences." He sat down. Hands were raised.

It was only the beginning.

Seven

It was late when Blue and Cassie arrived back at his house. Mavis had fallen asleep in front of the television set, but when they entered the house, she yawned. "How did it go?"

Cassie was still excited over the success of the project. "Blue gave a wonderful speech," she said. "Then we watched a film that showed how some of our elderly live. The crowd responded generously."

"Would you like a cup of coffee, Cassie?" Blue asked from the kitchen.

"Yes, thanks." She returned her attention to Mavis. "By the time the meeting was over, there was more than enough money raised to launch the project and enough volunteers to care for the shut-ins. Even Dr. Richardson from the clinic agreed to donate one day per month to check on them, and he promised to talk to his colleagues about getting involved."

Cassie reached into her purse. "Look, I even have a shut-in to visit. She's eighty-two years old and loves to read but has cataracts. Once I find out what she likes to read, I'm going to the library and—"

"Are you going to keep yakking or are you going to let Mavis go to bed?" Blue asked, holding out a cup of instant coffee to her.

"I'm sorry," Cassie said, seeing how tired the woman looked. "Did the girls behave?"

"Of course they did," Mavis said, pushing her tall frame from the couch. "They didn't give me any trouble. We played checkers and bingo and old maid." She yawned wide. "Well, g'night, folks. I'm glad your dinner was a success." Mavis made her way up the stairs to her bedroom.

"She's nice," Cassie said, once Blue joined her on the sofa. He had already slipped off his jacket and loosened his tie.

He nodded. Although he was tired, he felt too excited to sleep. He pulled off his shoes and propped both feet on the coffee table while he sipped his coffee. "Thanks for going with me," he said to Cassie, who had kicked off her high heels as well. Her legs were curled beneath her, and she looked very much at home.

"I couldn't believe the turnout tonight," she said. "The place was packed."

"That's only because they knew you'd be there," he said, a smile tugging his lips. "They wanted to see what New York's highest-paid model looked like after all these years."

"You know that's a lie, Blue Mitchum," she said.

"This town loves you. Sadie Ferguson said you had OSHA investigate the working conditions in the mill after you'd heard rumors. My parents work in that mill, Blue. They have all their lives. You may have made their jobs a little safer."

"Cassie—"

"And that's not all. While you were shaking hands, I learned just how much you've done for this community. Jeremy Bishop says you've done more in three years than most mayors do in ten."

Blue sighed. "Cassie—"

"All I'm trying to say is how proud I am of you," she said simply.

He looked surprised. "Really?"

She nodded enthusiastically. "I was so caught up in the bad-boy image you'd presented in the past that I couldn't see what a wonderful man you've become. You're caring and sensitive and—"

"Cassie, you're embarrassing me. It's my job, okay?" Inside, though, he was bursting with pride. To think Cassandra D'Clair, whose face had adorned hundreds of magazine covers, the same woman who had designers begging her to show their creations, was proud of him, was more than he could comprehend. She'd rubbed elbows with the ultrarich and the famous. And she was proud of *him*, a small-town mayor who ran a cattle farm and just made ends meet.

Blue suddenly reached into his shirt pocket and pulled out a folded check. He handed it to Cassie.

She recognized the check as her own. "Where did you get this?"

"The treasurer handed it to me before we left,"

he said. "Don't you think ten thousand dollars is a bit much to donate for a single cause?"

"I resent that," she said, setting her coffee cup down. "I wrote this check because I wanted to help buy a truck to deliver the meals to the shut-ins. It was a personal decision, not one that needed to be discussed by the committee. I should have given anonymously, but I don't make a habit of carrying that much cash with me."

Blue couldn't help but smile at the piqued expression on her face. "Cassie, this is a community project. I don't expect one person to carry the load."

She was silent for a moment. "Has it ever occurred to you that I might be repaying a debt?" When her words drew no response from him, she continued. "Look how I've been blessed, Blue." She paused and thought about it. "I was born into a family who loved me and saw that I had all I needed. We weren't rich, but we never did without. I had a very happy childhood with two wonderfully crazy sisters."

"But, Cassie—"

"Then I decided to go to New York to design, and what happened? I was thrust into the high-paying modeling industry." Her eyes clouded. "Sure, I had to put up with Jean-François, but he was seldom home. I lived in the most exclusive areas, traveled all over Europe and the Orient. I've done more in my thirty years than most people ever have a chance to do in a lifetime. On top of that, I have two beautiful, healthy girls. Ten thousand dollars is hardly enough to help those who are suffering, when I've had the best life could offer." She gave him a sly grin. "Besides, I'm rich. I can afford it."

Blue sighed heavily. "Cassie, that's beside the point. There will always be a cause in this town. I would rather you gave the same as everybody else. Besides, you're pouring a fortune into that house. The girls will eventually need money for college, and you'll need something to retire on. I can't accept this check in good conscience." He reached for it and tore it in half, while Cassie looked on in disbelief. "You did a good thing by volunteering to take on a shut-in. If you want to make a donation as well, that's fine. But be reasonable."

Cassie felt embarrassed. She had meant to offer all she could for the cause. Her gift had been sincere. Blue probably saw it as her way of flaunting her money. "I'll write you another check in the morning," she said quietly. She unfolded her legs and started to get up from the couch. "I think I should go to bed now."

Blue reached for her hand. "I didn't mean to hurt your feelings," he said gently. When Cassie refused to meet his gaze, he turned her face toward him with one finger. "I care what happens to you, princess."

"Please don't call me that, Blue," she said. "I'm not royalty."

"To me you are." Without warning, he pulled her onto his lap and looked into her eyes. The dim light made them a deep violet. "Cassie, I never thought I'd learn to care about another human being. True, I've done things to help the community, but that was just another cause I believed in as a concerned citizen. But you . . . and your girls . . ." He paused, trying to think of just the right words. "You've turned my life around."

His face was so close, Cassie found breathing difficult. There was Blue Mitchum telling her he cared about her. She certainly wasn't indifferent to *him*. She had always had a special place for him in her heart, but she'd told herself it was a childhood fantasy. Surely she hadn't fallen in love with the man. Or had she? "What happened to the hell-raiser I used to know?" she asked when she could manage to speak.

"We don't need to go into all that."

"Yes, we do. Otherwise, I'll keep wondering if you're for real or if this is some act." She had just confessed the truth, both to Blue and to herself. He had done nothing to earn her distrust. She was letting her failed marriage cloud her perspective.

He looked surprised and a little hurt. "It's no act."

"If you truly care for me as you say you do, you'll trust me enough to tell me."

Blue shoved her away gently and leaned forward on the couch, clasping his hands. It was as though he were trying to distance himself from her.

He reached for his coffee cup, drained it, and set the empty cup down on the coffee table. "It was big news when it happened," he said. "Nobody talks about it anymore. But I see it every time I close my eyes at night."

"What?" Cassie prodded gently.

Blue refused to look at her. "It was probably the worst automobile accident that ever occurred in Peculiar." He faced her, and there was a derisive smile on his lips. "I was still a troublemaking punk with no future. I hung out with the worst of them. Most of the time we were drunk and rowdy. Got into more fights than I can remember." He leaned back on the couch and crossed his legs. "Then one night several of my buddies and I got drunk and decided to race another car. The driver of the car I was riding in lost control and slammed into a telephone pole. I was in the back seat and was the only survivor."

Cassie heard a gasp escape her lips. "It must have been awful."

"Yeah. I lost consciousness for a couple of minutes, but when I came to, the car was twisted and smashed to hell. They actually used a chain saw to cut me out. I had to sit there and wait with my dead buddies beside me."

"Don't tell me any more," Cassie said gently. She touched his cheek. "How badly were you hurt?"

"I spent a few months in the hospital." He gave her a weak smile. "I think I broke just about every bone in my body."

"But you're okay now?"

"Yeah, I'm okay. I have a couple of small scars on my legs, but no big deal. They did a good job of sewing me up." He was silent for a moment. "Three months is a long time to spend in the hospital, you know?" When Cassie nodded, he went on. "It gives you time to think. For the first month I hated myself and wanted to die. I felt guilty for living. Then I began to wonder *why* I had lived. Surely there must've been a reason. Folks started dropping by to see how I was doing—complete strangers even. Some sat with me for hours. I was still bitter and refused to talk to them, but they kept coming. It was the first time in my life I felt anyone really gave a damn about me."

"What did you do then?"

"Once I was healed, I found a job and pulled my act together. No more booze. No more fighting. I decided to use my energies elsewhere. If there was a barn-raising event in town, I took part in it. When the Baptist church needed painting, I was there. After a while it became a habit with me."

"Blue?"

He looked at her. "Yeah?"

"I'm glad you lived." She leaned over and kissed him on the cheek.

His look was solemn for a moment before he broke into a slow, tantalizing grin. "I don't want you to think the accident affected my ability to . . ."

Cassie couldn't help the laughter that bubbled out of her. "The thought never crossed my mind."

"In fact, I think I've improved with age."

"I'm going to bed now, Blue," she said, standing. She could feel the warm blush on her cheeks. He stood as well, and there was laughter lurking in his eyes. "You know how it is when you're young. You tend to hurry things a bit."

"I don't want to hear this." He knew what he was doing to her, she thought. The time to escape was now.

"Once you get a little older, you learn to be patient and thoughtful." He followed her out of the room and down the hall. "You take it slow and easy. You make it last."

She was never going to fall asleep. "Good night, Blue," she whispered as she made her way upstairs with him looking on.

It was the coffee, Cassie told herself an hour later as she tossed and turned in her bed. Her silk gown twisted around her legs and frustrated her even more. She sighed, climbed out of bed, and stared out the window at the night. Stars filled the sky like precious jewels on a canopy of black velvet. It was funny how different the country was from the city, she thought.

It was funnier still how Blue Mitchum had turned her world upside down. But then, hadn't he always? Even at fifteen she had fantasized about the wild youth. There had been times in New York when she had wondered about him, but she'd blamed it on loneliness.

Cassie began to pace the floor, wishing the wood would not creak beneath her. Deep down she ached, and wondered at the feeling. She had never been kissed as Blue had kissed her. He could be gentle and loving or hungry and greedy with her. He was able to coax a multitude of sensations from her just by the gentle lull of his voice.

Warm milk, she thought, as she slipped on her robe. That's what she needed. Lord, she hated warm milk, but she would gag it down if she had to, in order to get her mind off the man sleeping in the bed downstairs. Cassie very quietly made her way down the steps, wincing with every creak. She fumbled through the darkness until she reached the kitchen and turned on the light over the stove. She opened the refrigerator and pulled out a gallon jug of milk, then located a small saucepan. This was not going to work, she told herself. She didn't need a glass of milk, she needed a drink. But Blue didn't drink, darn it!

Cassie sighed. She poured the milk into the saucepan and turned on a burner. Five minutes later the milk began to bubble. Cassie poured the hot liquid into a glass and sipped it cautiously. She made a face. It tasted awful.

Once she had drained the glass, she cleaned up her mess and started for the stairs. Suddenly she stopped. For a moment she was immobile. Her heart pounded. Her stomach fluttered as though wild birds had taken flight inside her. A roaring sound filled her ears. Then slowly she crept toward Blue's bedroom as if some magnetic force were pulling her. She paused just outside the door. It was inevitable, he had once told her, and now she knew it was the truth. She turned the doorknob and was thankful to find the room unlocked.

Cassie pushed the door open slowly. Moonlight streamed across the room in a wispy vapor. She stood there for a moment, staring at the man on the bed, then moved closer.

Blue blinked at the figure approaching him. "Cassie?" He raised on one elbow. With one fluid movement he swept the covers aside in a silent invitation for her to join him. "I've been waiting for you," he said. "For years," he added in a voice heavy with emotion.

Cassie gave a small nervous laugh. She was unaware of the picture she made with the moonlight bathing her face, highlighting the sheer folds of her gown and robe, and the wild hair that had paved her way to success.

"Don't be frightened," Blue said, his broad shoulders silhouetted in the moonlight. "If you like, I'll just hold you."

His compassionate offer gave Cassie the courage to climb in beside him. The sheets carried his scent, and the fragrance intoxicated her. She sucked her breath in sharply when he pulled her close and she discovered he was naked beneath the covers.

"Cassie, why don't you take off your robe?" Blue suggested, giving a soft chuckle.

"My robe? Oh, yes, I forgot." Cassie managed to shrug off her robe with Blue's help. He laid it aside and pulled her back into his arms. His long legs burned hers through her gown as she lay very still beside him. She was certain the pounding of her heart would wake the entire household.

Blue kissed her tenderly. Although his passion was rising rapidly, he kept it in check. The last thing he wanted to do was frighten her. "Touch me, Cassie," Blue prodded gently. "Touch my face."

Surprised, Cassie did as he asked, and stroked one cheek, finding it already rough with a light growth of beard. Blue framed her face in his hands.

"You're beautiful," he whispered, capturing her lips in another kiss. He moved her hand from his face to his chest, and Cassie delighted in the coarse texture of the hair there. His powerful muscles flexed beneath her touch. She slid her fingers lightly across his stomach, where the hair grew sparse.

"I like that," Blue whispered against her ear, his breath hot. He was already hard and aching for her, but determination made him take it slow. He had wanted to bed Cassie for as long as he could remember. If this were to be his only chance, he would woo her with sweet words and kiss her until she whimpered his name.

Cassie's head was spinning. She could feel Blue's hard length against her thigh, and a warmth filled her lower belly. Through the fabric of the gown, he stroked her breasts, one at a time, his caress no more than the whisper of a breeze on a summer's day. His gentleness was a welcome touch after Jean-François's painful one. But that was another life, she told herself. It no longer existed.

He lowered his head to her breasts and flicked her nipples lightly with his tongue, wetting the fabric of her gown. Once the hardened peaks were tight and eager, he moved his lips to the hollow of her throat and along each shoulder. As his lips skimmed across silken flesh, he pulled the dainty straps of her gown down each arm. When Cassie was naked to the waist, he stopped and stared at her in wonder. Even in the darkened room he could see that her breasts were perfect. The dusky nubs that had tightened from his kisses once again tempted him, and he toyed with each one until Cassie moaned with desire.

By the time Blue removed Cassie's gown, she felt as though she were climbing higher to some idyllic place filled with wonderful sensations. Her shyness drifted away like diminishing storm clouds and left her feeling as though she were bathed in sunshine. Blue began a gentle exploration of her body with his lips. He tongued her navel until she writhed in delight. His fingers stroked the inside of her thighs until she was certain he would start a blaze. Then he grasped one of her hands and brought it to him.

Anxiety suddenly gripped Cassie among the haze of sweetly whispered words and soft caresses. As though sensing her withdrawal, Blue whispered words of assurance in her ear. Suddenly she felt silly. She wasn't a blushing virgin, for heaven's sake; she was the mother of twins.

A thought occurred to her, although it had to fight its way past the feelings and emotions in her pleasure-drugged brain. Perhaps she wouldn't measure up to Blue's expectations. She had never learned the secrets that some women used to please a man. Her own experience with lovemaking had been one of frustration. Her body had never ached for a man. She had never known total pleasure, only violation.

Cassie's eyes flew open as Blue inched his way down her body with his lips. She stiffened when he moved between her thighs. "Blue?"

"Shhh, baby. Just relax and let me show you what it's like this side of heaven."

Blue's tongue sent flames through her that had her gasping. Once again she felt as though she were climbing higher and higher. Although it was wonderful and delightful, Cassie began feeling a discomfort, as though she couldn't quite get enough. The feelings were so powerful, she needed some sort of escape. Blue's fingers slipped inside her body teasingly as his tongue worked its magic on her thighs. Cassie stiffened.

"Let it happen, Cassie sweet," he whispered.

Suddenly her body arched and gave way to a sensation so powerful that she cried his name and grasped the sheets, half-afraid she would fall off the edge of the universe. Her body continued to pulse with desire as Blue worshiped her with his lips. When the feeling subsided, he brought it back, his tongue feather-light against her sensitive femininity. Cassie was weak and trembling. Nevertheless, she was ready when Blue entered her slowly and cautiously, filling her completely.

"You're so tight," he whispered against her lips.

"Blue, I've never—" she felt self-conscious about her own lack of control. Her thighs had stiffened, and she had raked her hands through his hair. She had never shared such intimacies with a man.

"I know, sweet. From now on you will. Am I hurting you?"

"No." Actually, it felt wonderful. She could feel his hard length against the satin walls that held him.

"Move your hips against me, Cassie. That's right, meet me." Blue muttered the words through gritted teeth as the silken lining chafed his manhood in a tantalizing way each time she arched against him. It was all he could do to keep himself from losing control. He moved against her slowly, reaching to capture her hips in his hands and anchor her to him. Before long, they were moving in unison. Blue began to thrust deeply, and Cassie accepted him eagerly. They both cried out at once, and their movements became frantic. Blue kissed her deeply as their bodies shuddered in delight.

Cassie felt as though she were waking from a dream as Blue held her in the crook of his arm. She could feel the steady rhythm of his heartbeat and knew it matched her own. Their legs were entwined, and coarse hair rubbed sensually against her smooth skin.

Cassie arose and reached for her gown and robe.

"What are you doing?"

She looked up in surprise when his husky voice broke the silence in the room. "Getting dressed."

He smiled and pulled her back. "No, you're not."

She welcomed the warmth of his body. "But I need to get back to my own bed," she said.

"In due time." He stroked her hair. "I want to look at you in the moonlight. You're beautiful." He paused, pulling her closer. "Cassie, what did our lovemaking mean to you?"

She smiled drowsily. "I never knew it could be so wonderful."

Blue smiled.

They talked and made love long into the night. Before it was over, Cassie felt she knew Blue, the *real* Blue Mitchum, as well as she knew herself. They lay there and watched the sky lighten into a kaleidoscope of soft hues before the sun's rays began to stretch its fingers across the horizon.

"I have to go," Cassie whispered.

"I know." Blue sounded resigned. "I'll walk you to the stairs."

Once they had both donned their robes, Blue followed Cassie to the bottom of the staircase. "Thank you," he whispered.

"For what?"

"For giving me the most precious gift I've ever had." He pulled her into his arms and kissed her.

It wasn't until Cassie was curled up in her own bed that she allowed herself to think about what had just happened between them. Blue had asked her what it meant to her. The answer was simple.

She was falling in love with him.

Eight

"Mommy, why are you acting so happy this morning?" Tara asked over a breakfast of bacon and eggs.

Cassie, caught in the midst of covering yet another yawn, was not prepared for the question. Her gaze automatically went to Blue. His look seemed to say: *I loved you pretty well, didn't I?* Cassie had forgotten for a moment how cocky he could be—not to mention smug.

"I'm smiling because Grandma and Grandpa will be back tomorrow," Cassie said. "Just think how wonderful it will be to see everybody." She took a sip of her coffee and gazed at Blue over the rim of her cup. "I'm sure Mr. Mitchum will be glad to have his house back to himself."

"But, Mommy, what about Pippin?" Tara asked.

"We'll miss him," Bree told her. "And you and Blue said we could have a kitten."

"Only if you have them fixed," Blue said.

Tara gave him a blank look. "Why, what's wrong with them?"

Cassie rolled her eyes. Mavis chuckled in the background. "Mr. Mitchum means we have to take them to the animal doctor for a simple operation so they can't have more kittens."

Tara wasn't even slightly appeased. "Why?"

"Because there are too many unwanted kittens around, that's why," Cassie said.

"Like with babies, right?" Tara added. "That's why they put babies and children in those homes . . ." She seemed to be searching for a word.

"Orphanages?" Cassie asked.

Tara nodded. "Only they lock animals in cages, right?"

Blue answered. "And if nobody wants them, they're put to sleep."

"Which really means they are killed," Tara said to Bree. "We're lucky we weren't put to sleep because Daddy didn't want us."

Cassie, in the midst of swallowing, spewed coffee on her robe. She coughed until tears streamed down her face. Blue looked at her in concern, but she wasn't aware of it. "Tara, what made you say such a thing!" she demanded.

The girl merely shrugged as though she had long ago accepted the fact. "Because it's true."

An uncomfortable silence followed. Even Mavis stood motionless at the kitchen sink. When Cassie spoke, her words were measured. "Tara, your father is a busy man. You should be proud that he's so successful. I'm sure he'd visit if he could. And you're wrong about him not wanting you. He loves you both very much." Cassie would have preferred biting her tongue off to standing up for Jean-François, but she wasn't about to let her daughters think they were unwanted by their own father. When she met Blue's gaze, she sensed approval and respect.

"Can we feed Pippin this morning?" Bree asked Blue, undaunted by the whole conversation.

"Do you think you can remember everything I showed you?" Both girls nodded enthusiastically. Even Tara acted as though any thoughts of her father had slipped her mind.

Blue relented. "Okay, then." The girls jumped up from the table. "And don't worry, I'll make sure your mother brings you to visit Pippin and the kittens once your grandparents return. You can each have a kitten when your house is finished." The girls seemed pleased as they let themselves out the back door. Mavis excused herself and headed upstairs to make the beds.

"You're something else, you know that?" Blue said.

Cassie looked up in question. "What makes you say that?"

"I would have exposed that worm for what he is."

"And end up hurting the girls? Should I tell them their father wanted me to abort the pregnancy from the very beginning? Never! I don't care how many lies I have to tell."

"They're going to find out what kind of man he is anyway." Inside, though, Blue agreed with her. He had known firsthand what it felt like growing up feeling unloved and unwanted. His earliest memories were of not being able to sleep without a nightlight. He'd been afraid of the dark. Instead of turning into a whimpering child, as he was certain his grandparents wished, he'd defied them. Anger consumed him. But what he hadn't realized at the time was that they'd managed to damage his self-esteem. He'd won it back by being the toughest hood in town.

"Perhaps they'll be old enough to accept it by then," Cassie said, breaking into Blue's thoughts. "I just don't want to see them hurt anymore. I want to raise them just as I was raised, give them a simple but happy life."

"Without a father?"

"They'll survive. There are single parents everywhere doing a darn good job of raising their children. At least here they'll have relatives who love them, and I'll have help if I need it."

"You've got it all figured out."

"I had it figured out long ago. It just took time."

They stared at each other for a moment. An uncomfortable silence stretched between them. Cassie was the first to speak. "Blue, about last night—"

"Last night was wonderful."

"Yes, but it was a mistake. I never should have come to your room." She whispered the last statement.

Horizontal lines creased his brow. "Why? We're both consenting adults."

She wanted to tell him the truth, that her feelings for him had turned into more than she'd bargained for. But how could she confess such a thing to a man like Blue Mitchum? Just because the earth had moved for her during their love-making didn't mean it had been the same for Blue. As far as he was concerned, it probably amounted to no more than a romp in the sack. He hadn't spoken of love or commitment.

But was she truly ready for either, she wondered. She had escaped the clutches of one man who had wanted to turn her into nothing more than a paper doll. Was she willing to risk her chance for independence after having been led around by an invisible chain for so many years? And was Blue willing to stick with one woman? She doubted it. She would rather die than spend her life as a mere puppet again. Nor would she lie in bed night after night waiting for Blue to come home. She and Blue might be wildly attracted to each other, but if the relationship failed, which she was certain it would, her girls would suffer again.

She would not allow that to happen as long as there was breath in her body.

"I came back with a specific goal in mind, Blue," Cassie finally said, deciding it was best to level with him. The last thing she wanted to do was lead him on. That thought almost made her laugh out loud. Her leading *Blue* on? Wasn't it the other way around? "As soon as the house is finished and the girls are settled in school, I plan to start designing my own line of executive women's wear. I already have contacts in New York who are waiting to launch the line. I've learned enough over the years as a model to do the job. As I said before, I went to New York in the first place to design, but got sidetracked."

"Why are you telling me this?" he asked simply.

"Because I don't need a man complicating my life."

"And I would do that?" He arched both brows.

"Yes. I would never know exactly where I stood with you. I could end up getting very serious about the relationship and—"

"And I'd crawl into another woman's bed, right?"

She refused to meet his stark blue eyes. "Something like that."

He chuckled. "Fraidy cat."

Cassie's head snapped up. "What?" He seemed to be taunting her.

"I thought you had more guts than that. I can't believe New York's hottest model is afraid of competition. I would have thought your ego much larger."

"I was never allowed to develop an ego," she snapped. "Jean-François taught me from the beginning that I was just another pretty face and without him I'd be a nobody."

"And you believed it?"

Cassie stiffened. She had said more than she'd intended. She had let Blue see the part of her that she had learned to keep hidden long ago. "If it were only me I had to consider, I wouldn't give a relationship with you a second thought," she said. She smiled to ease the tension in the air, but Blue's look was dark and foreboding. Her smile faded. "I'm not going to let you find your way into my heart, charm my little girls, and make me fall in love with you." Her gaze locked with his. "And risk the consequences," she added.

Blue gave her that smug look that always set her pulse racing. "Oh, so that's it. You're afraid you'll fall in love with me." He saw the rosy blush on her face. "You like the things I do to you in bed, but you don't want to go public with our relationship. Is it because you feel I'm beneath you? Afraid I'll be a bad influence on your daughters?"

"Don't start that again."

"I think you're just making excuses, Cassie," he said tightly. "Perhaps the thought of breeding with a savage is more than your delicate system can take."

Cassie felt as though she'd just been slapped in the face. "You know that's not true!"

He pushed his chair away from the table. "I don't know what's true anymore. Your excuses are flimsy as hell, and I don't have time to listen to them. I have work to do. Now, if you'll excuse me, your highness . . ." He saw the pained expression on her face as he let himself out the back door.

Cassie was miserable for the rest of the day. Blue seemed to avoid her except when the girls were present. His aloofness hurt after a night filled with lovemaking and tender, whispered words. She had made the right decision, she told herself. She had, as the saying went, nipped the relationship in the bud before it grew out of proportion.

Mavis prepared a dinner of country ham, broccoli casserole, and a pan of fried squash, potatoes, and onions. Both girls turned up their noses at the food, but Cassie insisted they taste each dish. As it turned out, they liked the broccoli, but no amount of ketchup could kill the taste of the squash and onions.

Afterward, Cassie bathed the girls while Mavis cleaned the kitchen. But Cassie's mind wasn't on the task at hand, and as usual, Tara noticed her mother was preoccupied.

"I'm just thinking about all the packing I need to do," Cassie said, wishing she didn't have to lie to her daughter. "After all, we leave tomorrow." She kissed both girls and tucked them in.

"You're thinking of Mr. Mitchum," Tara said glumly as her mother kissed her forehead.

Cassie froze. "What makes you say that?"

"You are always staring at each other," the girl accused. Jealousy rang loud in her voice.

Bree rose on one elbow. "Are you in love with Mr. Mitchum?" she asked hopefully. "Because if you are, then we don't have to leave, and Tara and I can ride Pippin."

"I am *not* in love with Mr. Mitchum," Cassie said, looking from one girl to the other. "Don't be silly. Blue and I are just friends, that's all."

Tara looked doubtful. "You said it was going to be just the three of us. That we'd be a team."

"And that's exactly what I meant," Cassie said. "We're going to have a wonderful life in our new house once it's finished." She looked at Tara. "Now, why don't you worry about little-girl stuff and let me worry about the rest?"

"Because I don't want to see you cry," Tara said, her bottom lip quivering.

Cassie's heart went out to her daughter. She took her in her arms and held her tight, wondering how the little girl had such insight. "Tara, listen to me," Cassie demanded in a gentle voice. "You and Bree come first with me. I'm always going to be here for you, even when you're all grown up." She smiled and ruffled her daughter's curly blond head. "Sometimes I think you're already grown up."

Finally Tara smiled and yawned, as though satisfied with her mother's answer.

"Good night, Mommy," Tara said, once they were tucked in. Cassie saw that Bree had fallen asleep the minute her head hit the pillow.

"Good night, sweetheart. I love you." Cassie turned off the lamp and slipped out the door, taking care to leave it ajar so the hall light would spill into the room.

She decided to remain upstairs instead of facing Blue again. She took a leisurely bath and washed her hair with a scented shampoo that she had personally endorsed. After towel-drying her hair, she slipped into a fresh nightgown. Once in bed, she tried to read the various books she'd packed, but none of them held her interest. She was concerned about Tara, quiet little Tara, who opened her mouth only when she had something staggering to say. Had the events of the past two years hurt the girl more than Cassie had realized? Suddenly Cassie felt very alone. She wanted someone to share her fears with. Independence was one thing, but having someone in your life who cared was important as well. Her thoughts automatically turned to Blue.

Finally Cassie closed the book and sighed. Her mind whirled with unanswered questions. And she wasn't fooling herself one bit. She missed Blue. That thought frightened her. All she had wanted to do was move back home and give her daughters a stable life. She had not counted on running into Blue Mitchum after all these years. She had certainly not counted on spending a night in his bed.

That was the last thing she needed to think about, Cassie told herself. Her muscles tensed at the thought of him lying naked between his sheets. His body would be warm and inviting. His hot mouth on hers would be sheer heaven.

As if in a daze, Cassie climbed out of bed and quietly headed down the hall toward the stairs. She paused at the bottom. Her heart was beating frantically. Lord, what kind of power did Blue Mitchum possess that could make her a physical and emotional weakling?

She should turn back, she told herself, even as she reached Blue's door and pushed it open. He was lying in his bed bathed in moonlight. He turned his head at the sound of the squeaking door.

"You knew I'd come, didn't you?" Cassie said dully, hating herself for her own weakness.

Blue didn't move, but merely stared at her. "No, Cassie. With you I never know what to expect." He sat up and held his arms out to her. "Come here."

Cassie was rendered helpless by the husky timbre of his voice. She went to him eagerly.

Suddenly they were kissing, their legs entwined, their bodies pressed together intimately. Cassie felt her head spin when Blue removed her gown and paid homage to her breasts. His teeth nipped each coral nipple gently; then he laved it with his tongue. Cassie shivered in delight. Her own hands were busy exploring the taut muscles on his chest and back. He smelled of soap and male flesh.

When Blue entered her, Cassie closed her eyes and gave in to the wonderful sensations. Leaning on his elbows, he framed her face with his big hands. "Open your eyes, Cassie," he said. "Don't shut out my face. I want you to know who you're having sex with."

"Blue, please . . ." Where was the tenderness he'd shown her the night before? she wondered as Blue thrust deeply into her, taking her breath away.

"It's me, princess," he said. "The half-breed. The bastard."

"Don't say those things," she pleaded, tears stinging her eyes. Her body was aflame.

"Why not? They're true. I want you to know precisely whose bed you're sharing."

Her cheeks were damp when she reached the glorious pinnacle. She climaxed with a force that left her breathless. Blue's climax followed closely behind, all pretense of gentleness gone from his lovemaking. When at last he had emptied himself, he rolled away from her and faced the window. He didn't see the tears streaming silently down Cassie's face as she slipped into her gown and crept from the room.

Blue cursed heaven and hell as he stared out at the night sky. He had hurt Cassie, the woman he had come to cherish in a short time. The woman he adored and possibly loved. Loved? The thought jolted him. He had never loved anyone in his life, and he didn't want to love Cassie. Nor did he want to be saddled with two little girls. Sex had always come easily to him. Even in a small town like Peculiar, there were plenty of eager women. He had always prided himself that he could more or less pick and choose his lovers. The last thing he needed to do was involve himself with a woman and her children. The sooner Cassie and her girls got out of his life, the better.

So why did he feel like punching a hole in the wall?

Cassie couldn't fall asleep. Had she not feared waking Mavis and the girls, she would have run a tub of hot water and scrubbed away all remnants of Blue's lovemaking. He had wanted to hurt her, despite wanting to have her in his bed. She balled her hands into fists at her sides until her fingernails threatened to break.

She had been right about Blue Mitchum all

along. He would charm and woo his victim, and once she succumbed, he was finished with her. Hurt and anger engulfed Cassie.

She had been a fool! And she'd let Tara down. Her eyes clouded with tears once again. Her heart ached. She climbed out of bed and crept into her daughters' room. She stared at their sleeping cherub faces and was filled with pride, then shame and remorse. Very gently she nudged Tara to one side of the twin bed and climbed in beside her. Her daughter made a sound in her sleep, and Cassie smiled to herself. She snuggled closer to Tara, basking in the clean scent that was so precious to her.

Cassie slept late the following morning, thankful she had Mavis to tend to the girls. She had lain awake until sheer exhaustion had taken over. When she awoke, she felt renewed. It would be her last day under Blue Mitchum's roof. Her parents were due back home, and she would rarely have to set eyes on the man. That knowledge alone would get her through the morning.

Cassie climbed out of the twin bed she'd shared with Tara, slipped on her robe, and slumped down the stairs in search of coffee. Mavis had a pot ready for her. "Sorry I slept so late," Cassie said, stifling a yawn. "Where are the girls?"

"With the kittens, where else?" Mavis answered. "I told them not to wake you."

"Thank you." Cassie hesitated. "Where is Mr. Mitchum?"

Mavis nodded toward the closed door to his office. "He's been locked up in there for hours.

Refused breakfast. Just had coffee." The doorbell rang. "I'll get it," Mavis said, already making her way down the hall.

At the sound of the doorbell, Blue pushed away from his desk and opened the door leading out of his office. He spotted Cassie sitting in her robe at the kitchen table, and their gazes locked briefly. She was the first to look away. He felt like scum.

Mavis appeared, looking somewhat unsure of herself. "Excuse me, Mrs. D'Clair. There's someone here to see you."

Cassie looked up in surprise. "Who is it?"

Mavis paused. "He says he's your husband."

Nine

For a moment, all Cassie could do was stare at Mavis. "Mr. D'Clair is my *ex*-husband," she corrected. Blue remained motionless nearby. "Are you sure that's who he said he was?" Cassie asked, feeling a sense of dread wash over her.

Mavis nodded. "That's what the man said. He has a French accent."

Blue had a dangerous look in his eyes that held both women's attention for a moment. "I'll get rid of him." His jaw was set in determination.

Cassie shook her head. "He'll only come back." She stood; then a thought struck her. "The girls!"

"Calm down," Blue said. "He isn't here for the girls. How is he going to take care of them, for Pete's sake?" He looked at Mavis, who stood waiting like a soldier for her orders. "Keep the girls out of sight," he told her.

"Not to worry," Mavis said. "I once had to hide my oldest boy from the law for three days. I'll keep the little ones in the barn."

"You never told me that," Cassie said.

"No time to explain now." Mavis was already heading for the back door, muttering under her breath. "I'll personally wring that man's neck if he so much as touches one of those babies."

Cassie took a deep breath. She was not prepared for a confrontation with her ex-husband. Her palms were damp as she headed down the hall dressed in her robe. She glanced over her shoulder and found Blue behind her.

"I'm coming with you," he said in a tone that left no room for argument. When they reached the front door, he opened it for her. Jean-François stood on the porch, a white limo waiting in the background.

Cassie saw that he looked older. The lines in his face had deepened considerably, and his shoulders sagged. For a moment they merely stared at each other. "What are you doing here?" Cassie asked without preamble. She was surprised at the tonelessness of her voice. During the months she'd spent fighting in court and waiting for her divorce to become final, all feelings for Jean-François had been wiped away.

He looked surprised but tried to hide it behind a broad smile. "You're looking well, Cassandra," he said, taking in the gown and robe. "I suppose it's this country air." He inhaled deeply. "Aren't you going to invite me in?" He looked past her to where Blue stood. "Who is this, your bodyguard?"

Cassie ignored the question. "What do you want?" she asked dully, surprised he no longer intimidated her.

Jean-François looked stunned. "My, my, is that any way to treat me? What would our children think?"

"*My* children," she corrected. "You never gave a damn about them, so don't start pretending. Now, back to my question. What do you want?" Cassie was aware of Blue's presence close behind her. He hadn't said a word. He was merely watching and waiting.

Jean-François crossed his arms and gave Cassie a stern fatherly look. "Well, for your information, I was recently notified that you were . . . How should I say it? Shacked up with some Indian."

Blue stepped forward. He was a good six inches taller, and his shoulders were twice the width of the older man's. "Watch what you say, Frenchy," he said between clenched teeth. "Don't want to get that new suit dirty."

"Hey, I did not come here looking for trouble," the man said, holding up both hands. "I'm just concerned about the welfare of my daughters."

"Like hell you are!" Cassie stepped forward. "You've never cared for anyone in your life but yourself. If you had loved the girls one iota, you would have demanded visitation rights in court. As it stands, I have sole custody, and I don't think it's in their best interests to see you."

Jean-François sighed heavily. "Why must we fight like this, Cassandra?" he said in a lulling voice.

"Why do you hate me so?" He didn't wait for her to answer. "Look what I did for you. I took some country bumpkin and turned her into one of the most famous models in the business. Do you think it was easy?" He gave a snort of a laugh. "You couldn't walk a straight line when I met you, much less model. And that Daisy Mae accent—"

Cassie stopped Blue from making a move. "Don't, Blue. This doesn't involve you. And he's not worth it," she said. She turned her attention back to Jean-François. "You were paid well for your services. Not to mention what you stole from me over the years. I supported your drinking, your women, and paid for your fancy clothes. I'm finished with you."

Jean-François's face turned a bright red. "You unappreciative little bitch! I wouldn't have gone looking for other women if you hadn't cringed in fear every time I touched you. I would never have married a frigid woman, no matter what the payoff. I should have let you rot in that menial job you had when I met you."

There was no stopping Blue. Without warning, he rammed his fist right into the other man's face. Blood spewed from Jean-François's nose, but Blue wasn't finished. "Perhaps you misjudged the lady," he said, holding the man by his lapels. "Frigidity is often caused by a clumsy partner."

"I see my information was correct. I had no idea my ex-wife preferred rutting with savages." His words fueled Blue's anger. Although the older man tried to fight back, he was no match for Blue. Cassie tried to pull them apart, pleading for them to stop. The chauffeur stepped out of the limo, looking confused. Blue's last punch left Jean-François lying in the dirt.

"Put this piece of manure in the car and get him the hell off my property," Blue told the driver. The man nodded, grabbed Jean-François under both arms, and began dragging him toward the limo. "Let's go back in the house," Blue said to Cassie, who was thankful to do just that.

Once inside, Blue poured her another cup of coffee and brought it to her at the kitchen table. "You're trembling," he said. "Are you okay?" She simply nodded and thanked him for the coffee. He took a seat next to her.

Cassie realized she *was* shaking. Had she really been afraid Jean-François would try to take the girls? Or was it the fact that seeing him again reminded her of the zombielike existence she had lived before divorcing him?

Cassie took a sip of her coffee. She forced herself not to meet Blue's gaze. She had gotten out of one mess, only to find herself in another. Not only had her staying at Blue's threatened his political career, she had fallen in love with those dark good looks, knowing deep in her heart it was hopeless.

"Why do you suppose that pathetic creature really showed up?" Blue asked, breaking into Cassie's thoughts.

She allowed herself to meet his gaze, despite the memories of the night before. "I supported him in style for eight years," she said dully. "Perhaps he has run out of money."

Blue was quiet for a moment, wanting to give

her time to calm down. Finally he spoke. "Cassie, I think we should talk." He had not slept the night before, and it showed in his face. He had felt like the lowest creature on earth after what he had done to Cassie, and now he was going to make it up to her if he had to crawl. "Cassie, I'm sorry. So very sorry."

Cassie shook her head. She wasn't about to forgive him and make him feel better. "I'm not up to talking right now. All I want to do is pack my things and get out." She stood, her insides feeling empty. Her mind played with images of the night before with Blue. Blue stood as well and reached for her arm. "Cassie, wait—"

Cassie shook her arm free. "Get your hands off me! Don't you *ever* touch me again, Blue Mitchum. Not ever! I'm tired of being used by men, and I refuse to let you use me. I'll be out of here as soon as I can. But don't you *ever* lay your hands on me again, do you understand?" It was a mouthful, more than she'd meant to say, and she had to stop and take a breath.

His features were tight. "I understand completely, *Mrs. D'Clair*." He saw the anger surface in her violet-blue eyes before she turned on her heel and stormed out of the room. A minute later, he heard her footsteps on the stairs.

Cassie was packed and ready that afternoon. She and Mavis had cleaned the house thoroughly, stripped the beds, and washed the linen, while Blue remained behind the closed door to his office. After lunch Cassie had finally reached her parents by phone.

Most of the luggage had been stowed in the back of Cassie's station wagon. Mavis remarked that only Princess Di would carry so many suitcases. "I hope those clothes are wash-and-wear," the woman added. "I hadn't figured on spending my twilight years standing over a sink doin' hand wash."

"I'll remember that when it's time for your pay raise," Cassie said with a grin, tossing the rest in the back seat. She'd grown close to Mavis in a short time and wondered how she had managed without her. The woman seemed like a member of the family. Although she and Cassie sometimes argued, it was all in fun.

Cassie glanced around the house for the last time and felt her throat swell with emotion. Had she done the right thing by breaking off with Blue? Had she really given the two of them a fair chance, or was she running scared again because of the feelings seeing her ex-husband had stirred in her? She was so confused. There was no room in her life at the moment for anyone but her daughters. They were what mattered, she told herself. But she couldn't shake the thought that she'd sacrificed something precious.

"Shouldn't we say good-bye to Blue?" Bree asked.

Cassie shook her head. "I think Mr. Mitchum is busy right now. Perhaps it would be best not to bother him."

"Coward," Mavis whispered.

"Meddler," Cassie retorted under her breath,

then smiled at the girls. "Besides, I left him a thank-you note."

"You're goin' to regret this day. I can tell when two people are in love." Mavis said it softly so the girls couldn't hear her. "If you ask me—"

"I didn't," Cassie replied as they climbed into the car.

" 'Cause you're scared of the answer, that's why." Mavis continued to ramble on, but Cassie's thoughts were elsewhere. Her heart was breaking. Now, as she closed the distance between her parents' house and Blue's, she wished she had had the guts to say good-bye to Blue.

Cassie pulled into her parents' driveway and was happy to see it filled with cars. Her sisters and their husbands and children were there as well. Mavis frowned at the scene. "Are you sure there's room for me here?"

"Of course there's room. My two sisters have moved out. You can stay in their old room."

When Cassie's mother opened the front door, she squealed so loud, it brought the rest of the gang running. Cassie could not remember having been hugged and kissed so much in her life. Tara and Bree were fussed over and coddled like newborn babies. It was a good half-hour before the commotion simmered down enough for Cassie to announce she'd come home to stay. Mavis helped prepare sandwiches and coffee, while Cassie told her family about the house she was renovating.

"But where did you stay all this time?" her mother asked.

"We stayed at Blue's house," Bree said.

Mrs. Kennard cocked her head to the side. "Who, dear?"

Cassie looked squarely at her parents. "Blue Mitchum loaned us his upstairs."

Silence filled the room. Mavis broke it. "We were very comfortable there," she said. "Mayor Mitchum sure is a nice man for letting us stay."

"You stayed there, too, then?" Cassie's mother said, looking a bit taken aback.

"Oh, yes, ma'am. Right upstairs with Mrs. D'Clair and the girls. I have never seen such a gentleman . . . so polite and all. 'Cept for my own kids, of course. That's the way I raised 'em to be."

Cassie's parents looked relieved, although her sisters tried to hide the smirks on their faces as they hugged her. "It'll be just like old times having you back," her older sister, Maggie, said. She whispered in Cassie's ear, "I'm glad you got rid of that snooty husband."

By the time everybody left, the girls were exhausted. Cassie and her mother put them to bed in the guest room while Mavis cleaned the kitchen. She insisted she was going to keep on doing her job no matter where she was staying. Afterward, once they had gotten Mavis settled in her room, Cassie sat on the front porch with her parents and discussed plans for the house. "I've been going by there every day," she said, "just to make sure the Suthers brothers are earning their pay."

"Do you plan to work?" her father asked, although he was smart enough to know Cassie didn't have to work for the rest of her life if she didn't want to.

Cassie smiled excitedly. "As a matter of fact, I do plan to start work as soon as I can get part of the house finished." She told her parents her plans, and they were impressed.

"What about the Frenchman?" her father asked, obviously referring to Jean-François. Her father had never made a secret of his dislike for the man. "Do you expect him to cause any trouble for you?"

Cassie decided not to tell them about the earlier unpleasant incident. "If I *do* have trouble, I'll slap a restraining order on him. He gave up his parental rights in court."

"You've grown up, Cassie," her mother said, taking her daughter's hand and squeezing it. "We're very proud of you."

Her father nodded. "And I plan to drive over to Mayor Mitchum's house first thing in the morning to thank him for taking in my daughter and granddaughters."

Cassie was thankful it was dark and they couldn't see the hot flush on her face. "Uh, I don't think that's necessary, Dad."

"Oh?"

She shifted uncomfortably in her rocker. "Blue . . . I mean, Mr. Mitchum and I got on well enough, but we had our differences. I think it would be best to just drop it."

•   •   •

Once Cassie had soaked in the old claw-foot bathtub that had belonged to her grandmother, she slipped on a gown and robe and said good night to her parents, who were getting ready for bed as well. In her room, Cassie picked up the stuffed animals she'd collected over the years and decided she would have to pass them down to Bree and Tara. She climbed into her bed and turned off the light. Her thoughts automatically flitted to Blue and their last night together. She still felt bitterly hurt, but she didn't blame Blue any longer. She had been as eager for him as the girls who'd climbed in the back of his station wagon years ago.

Over the next two weeks Cassie was as busy as ever. Bree and Tara had begun first grade, so Cassie and Mavis spent more time at the house, which was buzzing with activity. There was much to be done, and Cassie plunged into one project after another. Her furniture arrived. She chose fabric for custom drapes. She supervised the workmen and offered her assistance when needed.

She was excited about her house, but Blue was never far from her thoughts. She literally ran into him one afternoon in Piggly Wiggly, when she turned a corner too quickly and slammed her cart right into his. She would sooner have run into the devil himself. For a moment she was too stunned to speak. He looked just as she remembered, blue-black hair combed neatly in place, and those eyes . . . Lord, she'd never forget those eyes. She saw them each night in her dreams.

"Blue, what a surprise." Her mouth went dry. She forced a smile.

His look was cool. "Pretty rotten thing you did, Cassie," he said without preamble. "Leaving without saying good-bye." Damn, he'd missed her. She looked fresh and clean in a pair of crisp white walking shorts and a pink blouse. So damn feminine. He could feel that old familiar desire stirring in his loins.

Cassie dropped her gaze. Her heart had lodged in the back of her throat, although she knew that was medically impossible. "I . . . I left you a note of thanks."

"How are the girls?"

"Fine."

"Tara?"

"She's adjusting to school very well. They put her in an advanced class."

He nodded. "That doesn't surprise me. And Bree?"

Cassie laughed. "She's the same."

"I miss them." It dawned on him suddenly just how much he *did* miss them. All of them. He even missed the clutter and the noise and the bickering. But most of all, he missed Cassie. Damn, he had screwed up the best thing that had ever happened to him.

Cassie moved her cart away and smiled self-consciously as she reached for a can of peas. "They miss you too," she said. She rolled her cart a bit farther, and Blue followed.

"How's the house coming along? It's looking good from the outside." He reached for a jar of mushrooms. He had no idea why; he hated the things.

"Yes, the painters are really making progress. The inside is still a mess." Cassie reached for a can of sauerkraut, which she knew she'd never use.

"How about your job?"

"Oh, I haven't had much time to work on it, but I've sent off some preliminary sketches." She realized sadly that they were talking like strangers. Was this the same man who had held her against him in the moonlight? Was this the man who had taught her pleasures that she'd never known existed? She ached to tell him how much she'd missed him, how many nights she had lain awake thinking of him.

A feminine voice broke into her thoughts. "Well, it looks as though our mayor has a domestic side to him," Jenny Bowers said.

Blue looked as surprised as Cassie. "Hello, Jenny. You remember Mrs. D'Clair?"

Jenny's smile was cold. "How could I forget? The whole town is talking about her. We can't wait to see your house once it's finished. Of course, you'll put us simple folks to shame. I understand you had a visit from your ex-husband."

Blue and Cassie exchanged looks. It was obvious now who had contacted Jean-François. Cassie smiled. "Yes, I did. It's a relief we can finally be friends and let bygones be bygones. If he hadn't shown up, we would probably have spent the rest of our lives holding a grudge."

Jenny couldn't hide the look of disbelief on her face. Cassie glanced at her wristwatch. "Well, I have to run. The girls get out of school soon, and I have to pick them up." She let her gaze meet Blue's briefly and saw a thousand messages there. "It was nice seeing you again, Mayor."

Cassie rolled her cart to the checkout, aware that Blue and Jenny were still talking. She felt as though someone had taken a knife and pierced her heart. She felt dizzy and sick at the same time. Seeing Blue had affected her dramatically, but she told herself she'd have to get over it. Chances were that in a town the size of Peculiar, they were bound to meet from time to time.

The cashier was an old friend of hers from high school. "Are you okay, Cassie?" she asked.

Cassie managed to smile and unload her cart, pretending to be interested as her old friend gave her the latest gossip in town. Her hands trembled as she wrote out a check for the groceries, and her knees felt like rubber as she followed the bag boy to the car, waited for him to put the groceries in back, then tipped him.

Cassie cursed herself as she drove to the elementary school to get the girls. She had seen the look in Jenny's eyes. It was the look of an eager woman, a woman who would sell her soul for a night with Blue Mitchum. She knew that look because she'd seen it on her own face in the mirror. There *was* one difference between Jenny and her, however. Cassie had been naive enough to fall in love with him.

"Why don't we ever get to visit Pippin like you promised?" Bree demanded when she and Tara had climbed into the car, cluttering the back seat with their schoolwork.

"I've been too busy working on the house," Cassie said. "And I'm sure Mr. Mitchum is busy as well."

Tara gazed out the window. "I miss holding the kittens."

"Well, there are plenty of cats and dogs at Grandma's house for you to play with," Cassie said.

"It's not the same," Tara said. "Nothing is the same anymore."

Cassie was surprised by her words. "What are you talking about?"

Tara answered simply, "You stopped smiling, Mommy."

Ten

Cassie awoke early the next morning to squeals of delight coming from the twins. She climbed out of bed and slipped on her robe.

"What's all the commotion?" she asked her mother, who was already up and preparing breakfast in the kitchen. She was standing at the window looking out back, a smile on her lips.

"Where are the girls?" Cassie asked anxiously.

"They went tearing out of the house in their nightgowns," her mother said. "Blue Mitchum just pulled up with a horse trailer attached to his jeep. Looked like there was a pony inside."

At the mention of Blue's name, Cassie glanced expectantly out the window. Her reaction was obvious even to her, so she tried to cover it with anger as she headed for the back door. "I won't allow Blue to spoil my girls," she told her mother.

"Where in the world are you going?" Mrs. Kennard asked. "You can't go out to speak to the mayor dressed like that." The door slammed behind Cassie.

Blue had already led Pippin out of the trailer by the time Cassie arrived on the scene. "Just what do you think you're doing?" she demanded, arms akimbo.

He took in the sight of her and a slow sexy smile spread across his lips. "Have I told you how much I like that gown and robe? Seems I remember—" He let the sentence drop, but the look in his eyes told her exactly what he was thinking.

Cassie blanched. She was wearing the same gown and robe she'd worn the first night they'd made love, the very same gown Blue had asked her to wear when she decided to come to him. At the time, it had seemed so preposterous for him to suggest such a thing. . . .

"I asked you a question," she said.

"I'm merely giving the girls a gift." He looked from Tara to Bree. "I've been trying to sell this pony for a coon's age. If I don't get rid of him, I'm going to have to send him to the glue factory."

The girls gasped. Cassie rolled her eyes. "Oh, really, Blue," she muttered. "Must you be so dramatic? Especially in front of the girls?"

"It's true." He stepped closer to Cassie and whispered in her ear, "I've found three potential brides for him, but he won't go near them. Know what I think?"

"No."

"I think he's gay."

Both girls gasped again. Cassie stared at them in disbelief. "You know what that means?" she asked, her voice rising on each word. Both girls nodded.

"Kids grow up fast these days," Blue said.

"Obviously."

"But we don't mind, Mommy," Tara said solemnly.

"That's the most ridiculous thing I've ever heard," Cassie told Blue, her anger at him softening as she tried not to smile. "How much do you want for him?"

Blue looked genuinely hurt. "I wouldn't think of charging you. He's a gift."

"Then I refuse to accept," she said adamantly.

"Mommy!" Tara and Bree cried out in unison.

Blue strolled closer to Cassie while the girls held the pony's reins and talked with him like an old friend. "Perhaps we can work out a deal."

"I don't make deals with the likes of you, Blue Mitchum," she said, his nearness causing her insides to quiver. "However, I'm certain you have a list of women who would gladly exchange favors. Call Jenny Bowers."

"You're starting to sound jealous," he said, "but then, I like that, coming from you. Are you the possessive type too?"

"You're so smug."

"So you've told me. At least a dozen times."

"You haven't changed. You're still a conniving . . . low-down . . . good-for-nothing . . . scoundrel. And those are your finer qualities."

"I'm glad to see you still hold me in high esteem."

She clenched her teeth. There was no need to

stand in the yard tossing insults at him. "About the pony . . ."

"It's a gift to the girls, Cassie, plain and simple. I can't stud him out. Besides, he misses them just as much as they miss him. He refuses to eat."

"He looks healthy to me." Cassie dropped her gaze from those fathomless blue eyes to look at Pippin. Blue's presence made it difficult for her to breathe. "Then we accept," she finally said, as the girls jumped up and down.

"Don't you think you should thank Mr. Mitchum for his kindness?" Cassie asked. Both girls thanked him dutifully. Bree ran over and gave him a hug, which he returned.

Blue walked to the back of the trailer and closed the door. His jeans were worn and snug, Cassie noticed. A T-shirt molded to his wide shoulders. His blue-black hair was neatly combed, and he smelled of soap.

"Would you . . . uh . . . like to come in for coffee?" she asked.

"No need to feel obligated," he said, heading toward the door of his truck. His tone was impersonal. "I did it for the girls." He climbed in and started the engine. "See you around." The girls waved and called out as he drove away, the trailer bouncing behind him and sending a cloud of dust in its wake.

Cassie felt disappointment well up inside her. Rejection was a bitter pill to swallow. Darn the man! Just who did he think he was? He could have accepted her offer of coffee. She made her way to the barn to get the pony settled in.

Blue pulled into his drive and cut the engine on his jeep. He sat there for a while, cursing himself for not accepting Cassie's invitation. What was wrong with him, for Pete's sake? He'd been wanting to catch a glimpse of her the past few days but had turned down a chance to have a cup of coffee with her. He could have gazed into those unusual eyes of hers and looked at that begging-to-be-touched hair.

He wanted her too damn much, he told himself. He had wanted her since she was fifteen years old and had been considered jailbait. She had spoken of her teenage fantasies once. He had wanted to laugh at the time. Her fantasies couldn't have come close to his.

Why not just take her and be done with it? he asked himself. She was vulnerable and as attracted to him as he was to her. He could feel the sparks ignite every time they looked at each other.

Blue pondered the thought for several minutes before climbing out of his jeep and slamming the door. No, he wouldn't just throw her over his shoulder and haul her off as he was tempted to do. Her ex-husband had done enough damage of that kind. She might appear sophisticated and self-assured, but inside he knew there was an insecure woman who was doing her very best to rebuild her self-esteem. It was paramount that she succeed, no matter what he wanted personally. As usual, his timing was off.

But then, his timing had always been off as far as Cassie was concerned.

•   •   •

The sheets were tangled around Cassie's long legs, and although her windows were open, the bedroom was stifling. Impatiently she kicked off the bedcovers, sat up, and fumbled for a pack of cigarettes. She lighted one and coughed, despite the fact she hadn't learned to inhale yet. A thought occurred to her. People sometimes died smoking in bed. She was risking the lives of her family. Not that Cassie was worried about falling asleep. She would give up her entire wardrobe for a good night's sleep, but every time she closed her eyes, Blue's face came into focus, and her mind was flooded with memories.

Cassie donned her robe and slippers. She picked up her package of cigarettes and lighter and left the room. Silently she made her way through the living room, unlocked the front door, and stepped outside.

The night air was cool on her skin. The sky was clear, and a million stars winked back at her. How many times had she slipped out of the house as a child, she wondered. She'd solved many a problem sitting on the steps stargazing. Her dreams of designing had been born under such a sky. She puffed on the cigarette and made her way down the steps leading off the front porch.

The grass had been cut that day and smelled oddly sweet. The fragrance of honeysuckle permeated the air. Night sounds—crickets chirping their mating call, frogs croaking in the grass—soothed her frazzled nerves. Being outside in the dark had never frightened her. "It's easier for God to watch over you," her mother had said aeons ago. Cassie breathed the night air and strolled along the dirt road in front of the house, where the moonlight had illuminated a path for her.

Suddenly she knew she wasn't alone. Her sixth sense told her as much. She saw a red ember yards away and knew someone was watching her, someone who was smoking either a cigarette or a cigar. Her heart raced. Her skin prickled, and the hair on the back of her neck stood up. She headed back to the house.

"Cassie, don't run away."

The voice was as familiar to her as her own. "Blue." She turned and blinked in the darkness. She could barely make out a figure moving toward her. When he reached her, she merely stared at him for a moment. "What are you doing here?"

"When did you start smoking?" he asked, ignoring her question. "It's bad for you, you know." He took a puff of his cigar.

Cassie tossed the cigarette onto the dirt road, and Blue put it out with his boot. "I just started," she said. "Of course, the girls don't know."

"Stress?"

She nodded. "Yes. A lot of stress. The house, the girls, my career—"

"I know how to get rid of stress," he said simply.

She stiffened. "That doesn't surprise me. You should hang out a shingle." He chuckled softly, and the sound sent tiny shivers up her spine. "I have to go in now." She suddenly realized how ridiculous it was to be carrying on a conversation with Blue Mitchum on a country road in the middle of the night.

"Don't leave, Cassie," he said gently. "I sit out here every night hoping you'll come out. You used to do that as a girl, remember?"

Cassie stared at the handsome face silhouetted in the moonlight. "How did you know?"

"I watched you. Whenever you couldn't sleep, you'd either sit on the front steps or take a walk. I was usually returning from a party. I would park my car down the road, just about where my jeep is now—"

"You spied on me?"

"You could call it that." He tossed his cigar to the ground and stamped it out.

Cassie was speechless for a moment. "Why, for heaven's sake?"

Blue's smile was tender. "Because I was in love with you." At her look of astonishment, he grinned. "Of course, at the time I thought it was lust." He stepped closer. "But you were so young." He reached out and traced her full bottom lip. "I can't tell you how many girls I took in the back of my station wagon, all the while pretending it was you."

"Blue, don't." Cassie stepped back. His fingers against her lips, his very touch, was more than she could bear.

"Yes, Cassie. I loved you then, and I love you now." With one fluid movement he reached for her. She was powerless. As his arms folded around her waist, his lips captured hers in a heated kiss.

Cassie broke the kiss. "I'm not ready for this."

"You've never been more ready," he said. "Otherwise you wouldn't be sneaking cigarettes."

"You're one to talk."

He gazed at her in the moonlight. "Are you going to let one bad relationship ruin your chance for happiness?" he asked gently.

Cassie laughed. "Are you suggesting I have a relationship with you? I'd be a fool."

"We already have a relationship, pretty lady."

"I'm not in love with you, Blue Mitchum."

"Prove it."

"I don't have to prove *anything* to you."

"Let me make love to you again," he said in a husky tone.

Cassie's stomach dipped at the suggestion. "You're out of your mind. The last time—"

His fingers grasped both of her arms. "Last time was a mistake. I am truly sorry. Let me make it up to you." His eyes were compelling even in the moonlight. When Cassie looked as though she had no intention of going, he loosened his grip on her arms. "At least come to my place so we can talk." He shoved his hands in his pockets and sighed heavily, raising his face to the stars. "I can't keep going on like this. Missing you. Wanting you. Needing you."

Cassie was amazed at how calm her voice was when she spoke. "You've always gotten exactly what you wanted, haven't you, Blue? All you had to do was snap your fingers and the girls came running. I even fell for it and climbed into your bed eagerly."

"And it was good between us."

"You're pretty much an expert. I imagine it would be good with any woman."

"Not emotionally. I've never made love to a woman I loved, Cassie." He ached to take her in his arms. "That's why I shut you out that second night. I realized I was falling in love with you. Do you have any idea what it's like to love someone when you've never loved another human being in your life?" He didn't wait for her to speak. "It's scary as hell. You start realizing that you care more for that person than you do your own life. You realize you'd literally die for that person. I never wanted to die for anyone, Cassie. But I would gladly lay down my life for you and your girls."

Cassie realized she had tears in her eyes. His confession had genuinely touched her. Blue was not merely handing her a line; she could feel the love pouring from him. She stepped toward him, and he pulled her into his arms for another heart-wrenching kiss.

"I'll go," she whispered against his lips.

The ride to Blue's house was made in silence. Cassie was nervous. Her palms were damp. Blue parked, climbed out of the jeep, and came around to assist her. Instead of letting her step down, he swept her high in his arms and carried her toward his house.

Once inside, Blue didn't bother turning on a light. He walked straight to his bedroom.

Cassie knew she was lost. She couldn't fight her feelings any longer. As Blue placed her on the bed and gathered her into his arms, she knew she would never find a more beautiful and desirable man.

Blue began to make love to her slowly. Each touch, each kiss, was ultrasoft. Cassie shivered as his warm breath fanned her ear and his teeth gently nipped an earlobe. Soon his kisses became hot and frantic, sweeping her up into a vortex of passion. He almost tore her gown from her body as he sought her ripe breasts. She crooned when he took a nipple between his lips and toyed with it until it was tight.

"I love your breasts," Blue said, moving to the other one. "Your nipples are so sensitive when I kiss them."

"Is that good?" she asked, still dazed.

"For me it is. And since you belong to me—" He didn't finish his sentence as he captured both porcelain mounds in his hands and buried his face against them. Cassie's sigh was like music to his ears. He wanted to give her more pleasure than she'd ever experienced. For once in his life he was not worried about satisfying his own needs, but fulfilling his lover's.

Cassie had never known lovemaking could be tender and feel so wonderful at the same time. Blue's mouth and hands were like magic on her body, caressing, stroking, stoking a fire low in her belly. His desire knew no limits. There were no boundaries, no rules. Nothing was taboo. He kissed and laved her with his tongue in places that made her writhe and blush at her own response.

Cassie surprised Blue by rising and forcing him

flat on the bed. Her lips sought his nipples and she swirled her tongue around them. She was pleased when they tightened into nubs. She buried her face against his chest and was welcomed by the intoxicating scent of his body. His chest hair was coarse against her cheek as her lips glided down his hard stomach. She suddenly felt self-conscious.

"I'm a bit inept at this sort of thing," she confessed.

Blue felt his heart swell with love. "Oh, Cassie . . . everything you do to me is wonderful."

With determination, Cassie searched out the pleasure points of his body, and drawing on his own techniques, worshiped him with her lips until he rolled her over. When he entered her, she felt as though she had been consumed by him. They stared at each other in the moonlight, both at a loss for words to describe their intense emotions.

Blue began to move against her slowly, grasping her slender hips to hold her in place. He stroked her breasts, then toyed with her nipples. He gazed at her with masculine pride as she rolled her head back and forth and cried out his name. Just watching her sent him over the edge. They chanted the other's name as they shuddered in each other's arms.

"I love you, Blue," Cassie whispered as they drifted back to earth. Her confession had obviously stunned him, because he stared at her awhile, then kissed her as she'd never been kissed before.

"I've always loved you, princess."

Blue stroked Cassie's hair and waited for their heartbeats to return to normal. A frown dominated his handsome face.

"What is it?" she asked, rising onto one elbow. "Didn't I—"

"You satisfied me more than I ever thought possible," he said, as though reading her mind. "I'm afraid I let *you* down this time."

Laughter bubbled from her. "I can assure you that you did not."

His look was serious. "You don't understand, Cassie. I didn't use anything. I didn't take any precautions this time. Is it possible that you could become pregnant?"

Cassie's mouth flew open. She mentally calculated her monthly cycle. She was ripe. "Yes."

Blue covered his eyes with an arm. "I can't believe how stupid I was. This has never happened before. I just wasn't thinking. I'm sorry, Cassie. Really sorry. If anything happens, I'll take full responsibility."

Cassie was still in a state of bewilderment. "I know you will," she said softly. "But it's just as much my fault. I'm a grown woman. I wasn't thinking either."

Blue's expression was grim, and he refused to look at her. "You don't want to be branded for the rest of your life."

"What are you talking about?"

"If you had to give birth to a—"

Cassie hushed him by placing a finger over his lips. "Don't say it, Blue. Don't even think it. If I do get pregnant, I will not have you or anyone else putting a label on our baby." She smiled in the darkness. "Besides, I don't think I'd mind being pregnant at all." She didn't see the look of utter disbelief on Blue's face. "I enjoyed being pregnant with the girls. I consider pregnancy a license to eat."

"Cassie, you have totally lost me. What about your career plans?"

"Oh, they won't happen for months and months."

He turned on his stomach and rose on both elbows. "Your career is not the only thing you have to consider."

"Meaning?"

He frowned. "How are you going to live in a town this size with people knowing damn well whose baby you're carrying? Not only will it hurt your reputation, it'll put a stigma on the baby."

Cassie sat up in bed and folded her arms. "Blue Mitchum, I'm tired of hearing you put yourself down because of where you came from." She saw the surprise on his face. "Sure, you had it rough in the beginning. Sure, you were a hell-raiser. But the people of this town have obviously forgotten it, because they elected you mayor. Why don't *you* try to forget it?"

Blue was amazed that she could see right through him.

"It's not that easy, Cassie. I've carried it around a long time." He studied her. "If you are pregnant, I'll marry you."

"You'll marry me if I get pregnant?" she asked quietly.

"To save your name, hell yes," he said. "But I would have married you the moment you were of age if you hadn't run off and married that French bastard instead." He shrugged. "Of course, I never thought you'd accept, but I was prepared to woo you. In fact"—he paused briefly—"I'd be damned proud to marry you if you weren't pregnant."

Cassie swelled with pride. She reached for him. "Come back to bed, Blue."

"Not until I have your answer."

"Yes. I'll marry you." Cassie barely had the words out of her mouth before he swept her up in his arms and kissed her deeply. "What about your house?" he asked.

"We can still live there if you like. Our properties run together, so you'll have even more pastureland. Of course, we can live here until the other house is renovated.

His look softened. "I want to adopt the girls, Cassie. I don't want them to grow up thinking their father doesn't give a damn about them. Especially Tara. She needs security. Bree needs—" He paused.

"A firm hand," Cassie said, and laughed. They talked and made love way into the night. As the sky began to lighten, Blue swept her hair back and gazed into her eyes. "Tell me you love me," he said.

"I do love you," Cassie whispered.

"Say my name. My real one."

"I love you, Neil."

•　　•　　•

Cassie cried out as she pushed with the next contraction. Blue held her hands and whispered to her encouragingly. "The baby is almost here," he said. "Look in the mirror, Cassie."

Cassie glanced up in the overhead mirror and saw that the baby's head was visible. "Oh, Blue, I can't stand it much longer," she cried.

"Okay, I want you to push harder on the next contraction," the doctor said. "It's almost over. You're doing great."

The contraction hit, and Cassie's abdomen rose with it. Blue assisted her as she pushed with all her might. She felt the baby slide from her body and sighed her immense relief. Exhausted, she lay back and closed her eyes. The pain was gone. For a moment, that was all that mattered. She was vaguely aware that Blue had kissed her.

"It's a healthy boy!" the doctor announced. "And a big one too."

Cassie's eyes fluttered open. "A boy?"

Blue looked anxious. "Doc, are you sure everything is okay? I mean, has he got all his fingers and toes?"

"He's perfect," the doctor assured him. He laid the squirming infant on Cassie's stomach while he cut the cord. "We'll clean him up in a minute so you can see what he looks like."

"I can see," Cassie whispered. "He has his father's blue eyes and blue-black hair."

"When are you going to decide on a name?" Blue insisted.

"I already have. I want to name him Neil." Cassie touched Blue's face tenderly. "After his father."

Blue could feel the sting of unshed tears in his eyes as he gazed down at his wife and son. He would have to call Bree and Tara and tell them about their new brother. But right now he wanted to hang on to this moment as long as he could. It was the stuff memories were made of. "Have I told you lately how much I love you, Cassie?" he whispered in her ear.

She smiled before she drifted off to sleep.

THE EDITOR'S CORNER

This month our color reflects the copper leaves of autumn, and we hope when a chill wind blows, you'll curl up with a LOVESWEPT. In keeping with the seasons, next month our color will be the deep green of a Christmas pine, and our books will carry a personalized holiday message from the authors. You'll want to collect all six books just because they're beautiful—but the stories are so wonderful, even wrapped in plain brown paper they'd be appealing!

Sandra Brown is a phenomenon! She never disappoints us. In **A WHOLE NEW LIGHT,** LOVESWEPT #366, Sandra brings together two special people. Cyn McCall desperately wants to shake up her life, but when Worth Lansing asks her to spend the weekend with him in Acapulco, she's more than a little surprised—and tempted. Worth had always been her buddy, her friend, her late husband's business partner. But what will happen when Cyn sees him in a whole new light?

Linda Cajio's gift to you is a steamy, sensual romance: **UNFORGETTABLE,** LOVESWEPT #367. Anne Kitteridge and James Farraday also know each other. In fact, they've known each other all their lives. Anne can't forget how she'd once made a fool of herself over James. And James finds himself drawn once again to the woman who was his obsession. When James stables his prize horse at Anne's breeding farm, they come together under the most disturbingly intimate conditions, and there's no way they can deny their feelings. As always Linda creates an emotionally charged atmosphere in this unforgettable romance.

(continued)

Courtney Henke's first LOVESWEPT, **CHA-MELEON,** was charming, evocative, and tenderly written, and her second, **THE DRAGON'S REVENGE,** LOVESWEPT #368 is even more so. J.D. Smith is instantly captivated by Charly, the woman he sees coaching a football team of tough youths, and he wonders what it would be like to tangle with the woman her players call the Dragon Lady. He's met his match in Charly—in more ways than one. When he teaches her to fence, they add new meaning to the word touché.

Joan Elliott Pickart will cast a spell over you with **THE MAGIC OF THE MOON,** LOVESWEPT #369. She brings together Declan Harris, a stressed-out architect, and Joy Barlow, a psychologist, under the rare, romantic light of a blue moon—and love takes over. Declan cherishes Joy, but above all else she wants his respect—the one thing he finds hardest to give. Joan comes through once more with a winning romance.

LOVESWEPT #370, **POOR EMILY** by Mary Kay McComas is not to be missed. The one scene sure to make you laugh out loud is when Emily's cousin explains to her how finding a man is like choosing wallpaper. It's a scream! Mary Kay has a special touch when it comes to creating two characters who are meant to be together. Emily falls for Noble, the hero, even before she meets him, by watching him jog by her house every day. But when they do meet, Emily and Noble find they have lots more in common than ancestors who fought in the Civil War—and no one ever calls her Poor Emily again.

Helen Mittermeyer begins her *Men of Ice* series
(continued)

with **QUICKSILVER,** LOVESWEPT #371. Helen is known for writing about strong, dangerous, enigmatic men, and hero Piers Larraby is all of those things. When gorgeous, silver-haired Damiene Belson appears from the darkness fleeing her pursuers, Piers is her sanctuary in the storm. But too many secrets threaten their unexpected love. You can count on Helen to deliver a dramatic story filled with romance.

Don't forget to start your holiday shopping early this year. Our LOVESWEPT Golden Classics featuring our Hometown Hunk winners are out in stores right now, and in the beginning of November you can pick up our lovely December LOVE-SWEPTs. They make great gifts. What could be more joyful than bringing a little romance into someone's life?

Best wishes,
Sincerely,

Carolyn Nichols

Carolyn Nichols
    Editor
LOVESWEPT
Bantam Books
666 Fifth Avenue
New York, NY 10103

FAN OF THE MONTH

Tricia Smith

I'm honored to have been chosen as a "fan of the month" for LOVESWEPT. A mother of two children with a house full of animals, I've been a romance reader for years. I was immediately captivated when I read the first LOVESWEPT book, **HEAVEN'S PRICE** by Sandra Brown. Ms. Brown is a very compelling author, along with so many of the authors LOVESWEPT has introduced into my life.

Each month I find myself looking forward to new adventures in reading with LOVESWEPT. The story lines are up-to-date, very well researched, and totally enthralling. With such fantastic authors as Iris Johansen, Kay Hooper, Fayrene Preston, Kathleen Creighton, Joan Elliott Pickart, and Deborah Smith, I'm always enchanted, from cover to cover, month after month.

I recently joined the Gold Coast Chapter of Romance Writers of America and have made wonderful friends who are all well-known authors as well as just great people. I hope to attend an RWA convention someday soon in order to meet the authors who've enriched my life in so many ways. Romance reading for me is not a pasttime but a passion.

THE DELANEY DYNASTY

Men and women whose loves an passions are so glorious it takes many great romance novels by three bestselling authors to tell their tempestuous stories.

THE SHAMROCK TRINITY

- ☐ 21975   **RAFE, THE MAVERICK**
  by Kay Hooper $2.95
- ☐ 21976   **YORK, THE RENEGADE**
  by Iris Johansen $2.95
- ☐ 21977   **BURKE, THE KINGPIN**
  by Fayrene Preston $2.95

THE DELANEYS OF KILLAROO

- ☐ 21872   **ADELAIDE, THE ENCHANTRESS**
  by Kay Hooper $2.75
- ☐ 21873   **MATILDA, THE ADVENTURESS**
  by Iris Johansen $2.75
- ☐ 21874   **SYDNEY, THE TEMPTRESS**
  by Fayrene Preston $2.75

THE DELANEYS: *The Untamed Years*

- ☐ 21899   **GOLDEN FLAMES** *by Kay Hooper* $3.50
- ☐ 21898   **WILD SILVER** *by Iris Johansen* $3.50
- ☐ 21897   **COPPER FIRE** *by Fayrene Preston* $3.50